Everything Ends...

"Please don't go." She leaned her forehead on the nape of Thorn's neck. It was the most intimate moment he had ever experienced. His whole life had been violence and pain and death.

This hurt more than all of it.

"I must go. It's my final task. Live or die. The High Vestal must know the truth. I cannot do otherwise. I am finished hiding from the Queen. I am finished hiding from the truth, only to discover death hides from me."

"They will try to stop you."

"They will try.

BOOKS BY MARTIN WILSEY

Solstice 31 Trilogy
Still Falling
The Broken Cage
Blood of the Scarecrow

Solstice 31 Universe
Virtues of the Vicious
Shadows of the Sentinel
The Law of Lumina
Revenge of the Renders

The Vampire Conspiracy
Blood Heretics
Blood Sky Dreams *

Short Story Collections
Peck's Halfway
Six Years Out

Anthologies as Editor
Silence of the Apoc
Whispers of the Apoc
The Witness Paradox

** forthcoming*

PECK'S HALFWAY

THE STONEBRIDGE TALES

MARTIN WILSEY

Peck's Halfway

ISBN: 979-8-89719-050-8 (Paperback)
ISBN: 979-8-89719-051-5 (Hardback)

Published by Tannhauser Press
www.tannhauserpress.com

Edited by Donna Royston
Interior Design by David Keener

To Joe Kirk.

Let's throw darts soon.

Contents

THE ONCE DAMNED

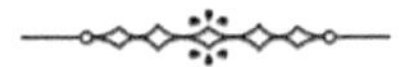

I. BLOOD IN THE SNOW

When all was quiet again, Thorn realized the blood dripping from his chin wasn't his. The blood looked black in the moonlight on the knee-deep snow. The light made it bright enough for him to watch the remaining two men ride off at a gallop, taking with them the horses of the six people that lay dead at his feet.

The next sound was always the same. A creak of leather as he squeezed the grips of his swords. They had saved his life again. Blades like no other.

They were perfectly matched staghorn grips, wrapped in fine leather.

The snow was thick on the tall pines that covered the region. The hush in the air consumed the sounds of the fleeing horses.

With a well-practiced motion, Thorn wiped the blood on his red sash and sheathed first one sword and then the other. He was careful of the crossbow bolt protruding from his chest, just below his left collarbone. He reached up and broke it off, leaving a few inches protruding.

"It was a good ambush, gentlemen," he said out loud to the dead.

Thorn thought, Waiting here at the Elder Bridge was the perfect place. I had to cross here. The trees provided ideal cover on the western side of the bridge. No footprints in the snow anywhere. Perfect. The Queen must be getting tired of losing so many men.

He looked over the edge of the thousand-year-old bridge as he leaned briefly on the stone wall. Assigning one of you to shoot the horse out from under me and then the rest to shoot at me as I fell was an inspired plan.

He began searching the dead, collecting coin purses, which he stashed in his black tunic. As he moved, he adjusted the curved swords in his belt. The staghorn made his elegant curved swords look like the tools of a simple farmer.

You should have left me where I fell in the snow for a few hours before approaching. Then filled me with more arrows before getting close. If you knew who I used to be, you should have been more careful.

As he took the last purse, he noticed this man had a flask on his belt. That's when he also saw the bolt that was in his own leg. The fletching was all the way through his thigh. Thorn felt around the back, and the wicked blades of the arrow had cut all the way through. He broke off the fletching and then without hesitation he pulled the shaft all the way through his leg. Blood flowed freely, and steam rose from the wound. Once again, he wondered where all the blood and magic that made it came from.

He took a long pull from the flask he had taken

from the body. It was a strong liquor that tasted faintly of apples. Thorn moved along and took his saddlebags from the dead horse and carefully draped them over his right shoulder.

These wounds would not close quickly out here in the cold wind.

He began to walk.

The eight horses had plowed a path for him down the middle of the road. As he walked, he could feel the magic sustaining him. It was like heat from within. The stars and moon were bright on the snow. The pines that lined the road were undisturbed.

He moved. The magic burned. His breath made no clouds in the cold. Anyone that was sensitive to magic would see him. They would feel him coming. There was no more hiding on this journey. Thorn thought he could see the distant light of the Keep on the horizon.

II. Peck's Halfway

The tracks didn't divert from the road, and just after midnight, he rounded the corner to the familiar sight of a large, multi-story inn made of stone, Peck's Halfway. He paused at the open gate and looked north into the darkness to see the distant fire in the Keep's watchtower.

From here, it was a day's ride to Bullard down into the valley in one direction and Rockriver in the other direction, back over the Elder Bridge.

He followed the tracks in the fresh snow through the massive stone arch into the courtyard where they led to the stables. No one else was traveling on a night like this. Thorn was backlit by the waist-high flames in the raised fire pit in the center of the large, walled, courtyard when the stable boy noticed him. He was young and frightened but approached anyway. The boy's breath came out in great gouts of mist.

Thorn stood motionless, seeming not to breathe at all.

"Good evening, mmm, my Lord. Can I be of service?" The boy said in a well-practiced manner. His voice only trembled a little.

"How long ago did those horses arrive? How many men were with them?" Thorn asked in a quiet growl, trying not to frighten the boy.

"Eight horses and two men. About four hours ago." The boy glanced down at the pool of blood forming at Thorn's feet, reflected in the firelight.

"Is Peck at the bar?"

"Yesss, sir," he stammered.

"Take extra good care of those horses, lad. And throw ten more logs on this fire for me." Thorn flipped the boy a coin. Its gold glistened in the firelight as he caught it. "I'll be back out in a few minutes." When the boy looked up from the coin, Thorn was already moving toward the main door of the inn.

Blood trailed behind.

Thorn could see that no one noticed the inn door open or close.

There was an outer entry that kept out the wind and maintained the heat. The drop in temperature within the room is what made people finally look up and notice the man standing in the entryway. The cold was not from the snow.

The common room was large and crowded with about sixty men and women, plus a few children. Travelers, going both east and west, stopped at Peck's Halfway. It was always busy. Peck had many suites, rooms, and bunks of all kinds and costs for them. As Thorn scanned the room, the conversations fell silent.

Thorn heard a ten-year-old boy mutter, "Papa, that man is bleeding." He pointed at the puddle growing at his feet.

A woman whispered, "It's him."

Another quietly uttered, "Magic," and averted her gaze.

Thorn's eyes locked on two men in the back of the room who were bent over mugs of ale. After a minute, he turned his back to them to face the bar.

Peck himself was there. He was fat with a bush

of curly hair on his head. Peck was clean shaven and missing a couple of teeth on one side of his mouth. He wore a white apron, stained with food. Peck was close enough to see the broken stem of the bolt sticking out of Thorn's chest.

"For the love of stone." Peck quietly cursed, "Please, Thorn. Don't destroy my inn again."

"Whiskey." Thorn requested, his back still to the people. The murmurs began behind him.

Peck was terrified. He was trembling as he set a large pewter mug, meant for ale, in front of Thorn and poured a half a bottle of strong brown liquor into it. He left the bottle on the bar and stepped back.

Thorn studied Peck's face as Peck watched two, tall, hard looking, well-armed, men walk up behind Thorn as he drank deeply from the cup.

"Please, Thorn. Not again," Peck begged quietly.

They stood a pace behind Thorn. One of the men was looking at the floor. "You're bleeding," he growled.

Thorn knew Peck had a small touch of talent. Peck could see the magic rising from Thorn as if his blood was made of molten iron.

He emptied his mug and dropped a fat purse on the bar. To Peck, he said, "For the mess."

Peck had backed up until he was pressed against the shelves behind him. "No, please. Not in here, not again," Peck whispered.

Thorn turned slowly to face the men.

"Peck would rather I die outside if you don't mind." He turned and limped to the door he had just come in, leaving the two men looking at each other for a moment.

When they exited, Thorn was standing in the courtyard with his back to the roaring fire pit. The fire was taller than Thorn, half again as high above his head now.

The two men slowly approached, separating a bit as they came closer. Their stances spoke of experience and formal training. Royal Army training.

Thorn reached up and released the clasp on his soaked, thick, wool cloak. It fell off his shoulders to the ground into the blood that was already collecting there. He stepped forward a pace and waited. His hands were relaxed at his sides. His mind drained to empty.

Faces were crowding the windows, and those that were brave enough to come to the door could see his leg and the left side of his body were slick with blood. They could see the remains of the shaft in his chest.

Thorn didn't move as the two men drew their swords. They stalked closer and closer to him. Their breath was creating clouds. The closer they got, the more Thorn seemed to grow still. His breath made no cloud.

When they were only two paces away, both of the men quickly raised their swords to strike at the same time.

Then Thorn moved.

Thorn drew his sword and struck in the same motion as he suddenly crossed the distance. The man on the left was cut in half diagonally by an upward cut, from ribs to opposite shoulder; the man on the right was suddenly headless--both dead with one strike while he drew the sword.

Thorn was frozen again like a statue at the end of the single stroke. He waited until the bodies fell in slow motion. His sword swirled again in a lightning-fast arc, the blood painting a line in the snow as it flew away.

Then he stood at ease and clasped the red sash that was tucked into his simple leather belt. In a smooth motion, he cleaned the blade and sheathed it.

When he began to walk back to the inn, people fled from his path as if he was on fire.

Peck was pouring the remains of the bottle into his mug as he returned to the bar.

After he had taken a long pull, he asked, "Do you still have decent whores, Peck?"

He nodded but didn't speak.

"Can any of them sew?" He emptied his mug. "I need a room with a hearth, lots of firewood, and your best wound wench."

Peck called out, "Thomas! Please, take Master Thorn to suite number four and then get Cass." A wide-eyed boy came up to Thorn's elbow, looking at all the blood on the floor. Peck set another full bottle on the bar. Thorn took it along with his mug and followed the boy.

"Lead the way, lad, before I fall down and embarrass myself," Thorn said and then drained the mug.

Thorn waited in one of Peck's best suites, thinking about the Queen.

The door opened, and a woman entered, carrying a tray of medical supplies. Her long brown hair was pulled back and tied with a leather thong at the nape of her neck. She wore a simple brown tunic with a thick rope belt.

She closed the door and turned to see Thorn standing in front of a roaring fire, leaning on the mantle. His shirt had been torn off and was hanging about his waist by his belt. She had never seen muscles like this before. His body had no fat. His skin was so thin she could see the textures of the twisting strands of individual muscles. Thorn sensed by her reaction that she could also see the heat of the magic rising off of his entire body.

"Good. You're here." Thorn said as he raised his left hand to grasp the mantle and lean into it, steeling himself. He drank the remaining contents of the heavy mug.

In a sudden flash of movement, he pounded the bottom of his massive pewter mug onto the bolt's shaft, and the cruel arrow blades burst from the back of his shoulder. His knees nearly buckled from the pain.

Cass almost dropped the tray.

Thorn took in a ragged breath and said with exaggerated politeness, "Would you mind pulling that the rest of the way out? Soonest?"

She set the tray down on the table, and, instead of going to him, she opened the door and called out for Thomas. "Bring food. Bring bread, cheese, soup, and eggs, stew and fried potatoes for six. Quickly, boy."

Thorn was still leaning on the mantle, with both hands now. He looked at her over his right shoulder. His chin rested on his right forearm.

Cass quickly walked over and added two more logs to the already tall blaze. She worked around where Thorn stood.

Standing, and without warning, she pulled the shaft out of his shoulder and threw it into the fire. "My name is Cass," she said.

He took in a shuddering breath. "Thank you, Cass," he whispered. "My name is Jacob Thorn. I'm…"

"I know who you are. You're the bastard who lived." She spat the words like an insult. She had produced a small, razor-sharp knife from somewhere. She began cutting off his clothes. He remained leaning on the mantle with both hands. Blood and magic were flowing anew. Despite the fire, the room was cooling, the very warmth being drawn out of the room by the magic that sustained him.

She removed his belt and set it with his swords on top of a large chest. She paused for only a moment and looked at them.

The rags of his shirt and pants went onto the blazing fire and were quickly consumed.

He stood there naked, covered in blood as she washed him from a large pitcher and basin.

"You are a fool," she said. "People don't hate you enough already? So you wander the countryside murdering people? And letting them see magic burning from you?"

There was a knock at the door. Thomas was there with a large tray piled high with food.

Cass took the tray and dismissed the boy. She walked over and set the tray on the same trunk as the swords. She lifted a pitcher of milk and added some to a hot bowl of soup. She took the soup and handed it to Thorn. "Drink this, all of it. Now. Before you freeze the inn solid."

He took his hands off the mantle and took the bowl. She added more wood. "You've done this before?" he asked. "You know how the magic works."

"Fools!" She started ripping up a loaf of bread into another bowl and poured more milk over it and then handed the entire milk pitcher to him. "Drink this. If you want these wounds to heal proper without freezing us out of this room."

He handed the empty soup bowl back to her as she brought him a wooden chair so he could sit in front of the fire. After he had emptied the jug, she took it to the door and called Thomas again. "Another pitcher of milk, more hot water, and clean rags, please, Thomas." He was off at a run.

Cass handed him the bowl of soggy bread with a spoon. "Now this." She dragged a table over from the wall and placed on it her sewing materials and medical supplies.

Thorn looked at the tray as he ate mechanically and noticed her face for the first time. She had scars there. Slave scars. Deep X's had been carved in each cheek. She must have once been a disgraced noblewoman: her posture and manner were not that of a slave. She must have been marked and sold into slavery.

She took the empty bowl from him and added another log to the fire. "That's enough for now." The room was still cold. "I will close this one first," she said, turning his shoulders to the light.

She quickly threaded a curved needle with a long fine black thread. Without hesitation or apology, she closed the X-shaped wound. "What was that in the courtyard? I have seen men die by the sword many times. I have never seen that before."

"It's called Masidill. The art of the draw." He paused, thinking. "It is a war art that is the beginning and also the end of a duel. Draw and Strike, powerfully, all in one. I may be the last of its masters."

She had finished his back and was starting on the chest when Thomas knocked. "Come," she called out. "Good. Thomas, I want you to help me. Wet a clean rag and gently wash his back where I have finished." Thomas did so without a word of complaint. Thorn was stoic and watchful as Cass applied medicines directly into the wound before sewing it closed.

More scars for his own collection.

As she worked, he examined her skin closely. Whipping scars peeked out from the collar of her tunic. Rope burn scars on her neck. Small wound scars here and there told a story of pain.

She finished sewing the front wound under his collar bone, and Thomas repeated his cleaning there. The boy was not afraid and not squeamish at all. He was firm and gentle at the same time.

Thorn had a gash in his ribs that he didn't remember feeling until now.

"I have never seen swords like those. But I have heard the legend of rune-marked blades like them. Made by a country blacksmith. Somewhere. No one knows."

It took almost fifty stitches to close that one. The white of his rib bones was exposed. "The story is true," Thorn said. "A country blacksmith and more. He told me this was the seventh set he had made. His best yet." Thorn winced for the first time. It was obvious he kept talking to distract himself from the pain. "After… I wandered for years, thinking I would never hold a blade again. Until I met him."

Thorn watched Cass kneel before him to close

the wound on the front of his thigh. His nakedness was apparently not off-putting to Cass at all. Not even noticed. Thorn's genitals were covered in blood, and Cass washed even there with clinical indifference.

"Thomas, draw the blankets down on the bed. I will need him lying face down to work on his leg." She helped Thorn up from the chair. His skin was clammy and cold even though he was so close to the fire. He slowly moved to the bed and lowered himself onto it.

This wound was ragged. Cass had to remove some torn flesh with her knife before she could sew him up.

He never made a sound.

When he was all clean and bandaged, Cass propped him up in bed and fed him stew, hot spiced apple sauce, eggs, bacon, and fried potatoes with onions while Thomas mopped up all the blood from the floor and stoked the fire.

"Why did you come here? Who were those two men?" Cass asked as she fed him.

"There were eight men."

Cass froze as the fork was halfway to his mouth.

"No more will come. The other six did this to

me, at the Elder Bridge. Had that arrow found my heart or I had lost my head, all the magic in the Kingdom would not have saved me."

Cass remained motionless as he spoke. Finally, she fed him the last of the eggs. She half-filled his mug with water and then upended a paper tube of white powder into it and then stirred it with her knife.

"Now drink this." She held it out to him. "It will help you sleep."

Thorn took the mug and paused a long time. He was looking into her eyes when he said, "Thank you, Cass."

He drank it all.

III. Warm Again

Thorn woke in darkness and realized he was finally warm. He was on his side facing the hearth. His injuries ached, but the medicines she had given him in the wounds and in his food had dulled the pain.

The fire had burned down to a deep bed of red coals. Thorn could feel the heat of them from across the room. He would live. Again.

He felt her move.

He was suddenly acutely aware of her. She was naked. His back was to her front. Their legs were tangled, and her hand rested on his hip. She snored quietly. The thick mountain of quilts held in their warmth. He was no longer drawing energy from the air around him to fuel the magic.

With a deep sigh, he fell back asleep.

When next he woke it was because of the sound of more wood being added to the fire. He looked, and he could see Cass in the growing firelight. The silhouette of her naked body was beautiful. She stood and arranged the fire with the poker, and as it flared, he saw more scars. Whip scars covered her torso. As she added and arranged wood she turned, and he could see burn scars on her breasts and cruel rope scars on her neck and wrists. Thorn had rarely seen a body with more scars than his own.

He had closed his eyes before she saw him awake. She walked around and slid back into bed, and slowly her fire-warmed body was all along his. Gently, she laid her hand on his forehead to check his temperature.

He opened his eyes.

"Fever?" he asked.

"No. The magic's chill is over," she whispered. "You are done drawing energy from the world around you. The magic is done with you. For now."

He raised his right arm so she could rest her head on his chest. "Rest now," he said.

He felt her fall asleep in small twitches. Holding her seemed to push out all other thoughts and pain as if it was a healing magic all its own. He quickly followed her in sleep.

The light in the window woke him the next day. He had lost track of time.

Thorn knew that Peck's Halfway was in a mountain pass and had steep cliffs on almost all sides. If the light was shining down here, the morning must be almost gone.

Cass had her back to him now. The quilts remained heavy on them, and he was in no rush to arise. She stirred, sensing him waking.

"I can tell you're feeling better," Cass murmured as she hugged his arm that was wrapped around her.

Thorn realized that his erection was pressed against her. Instantly embarrassed he turned from her. "Forgive me. It's just…"

"It's just that you're feeling better." She hugged his back. "I have not slept that well in ages. Thank you, Jacob. May I call you Jacob?"

Thorn had a flash in his mind of an ordinary life. Waking on a winter morning with a woman he loved. Lingering in a warm bed as long as possible. Then reality rushed back in. There would be no love for the damned.

"What's wrong?" Cass was more sensitive than he had realized.

"Nothing. Don't worry. I won't hurt you. I promise."

"I know you won't hurt me. No one will hurt me ever again. I have already had my lifetime's worth."

"I saw you. In the firelight." He rolled onto his back, and she once again placed her head on his chest. His right hand traced the scars on her back. Some were raised and coarse. Some were divots or trenches in her skin.

"Peck got me for a bargain," she frowned. "Is that what you mean?"

Thorn considered what to say before speaking.

"I think I am going to sleep every night, in this bed, for the rest of my life," Thorn said. "With you."

"Ha!" she barked. "You plan on buying me from Peck?"

"I think I will." He was suddenly serious. "I have more than enough gold I won't need. It will only be one more night. Then I will go off to my well-deserved death."

"You are not considering going up to the Keep? They know who you are. They will already know you are here." She sat up and looked into his eyes. "Those men… were probably from there."

"Cass, I was the King's Guardian. I swore an oath, a magic oath, on penalty of curse, of doom, to protect the throne or die trying."

There was a long pause.

"I lived."

"So you've been trying to die honorably ever since?" she said as if it was all folly.

"The Gods have not made it easy. Once damned, they enjoy drawing it out, it seems," he said and looked at the fire.

"Gods be puke. Just go," she pleaded with him. "Find a quiet life somewhere. Don't be Royal Guardian, anymore. Walk away."

He petted her hair. Finally, he just sighed and

said nothing.

"Please, Jacob. Just live. What good would vengeance serve? Please. I just finished putting you back together." She was about to cry.

"I was serious, you know," he said quietly. "I'll buy you from Peck. You are already free. Whether I go to the Keep or not. You will be free." He looked into her eyes, trying to discover why she would care. "I can at least do one final kindness for the world."

"Jacob, please don't go up there. They have great power. Magic, science. The Queen may even be there. The least of their weakest girls can read and brew a poison that could kill us all. The greatest of them, the High Vestal, they say, was the hand behind the death of the King."

"I know. It is why I must go." There was sadness in his voice.

"You have no honor any longer. You're truly damned already. What do you owe the world? Don't be a fool." She climbed out of bed and angrily began to dress. "I cannot send someone to his death unhealed or hungry, damn you."

She was flushed, angry. "I will bring food and check your wounds. And…"

"Wait," he said and reached out a hand to her. It was like gravity. She took it. "Let me tell you what happened. One person at least should know the truth of my oath breaking."

She sat fully dressed at the edge of the bed.

"How much of the story do you know?" he asked.

"It was the funeral of Prince Gareth." Cass replied. "It is rumored he was poisoned. Not simply drunk and choking on food. The King attended with his six personal guards, including you, and the entire Prince's Honor Guard was there." She swallowed. "Once inside the Cathedral the doors were locked from the inside. And only you survived the day. Sworn to give your life before his. The King was killed, and you walked away in disgrace." She paused, looking at their hands. "Loyalists have been challenging you to duels ever since."

"It was sixty against six." He closed his eyes, seeing it repeat as in his dreams every night. "They had crossbowmen in the balcony. They didn't know that we six could strike bolts from the air. They didn't know we had been spell cast, giving us enhanced physical speed, perception and the ability to survive massive, even lethal wounds for a while."

Thorn opened his eyes and met hers.

"I lived. I should have fallen on my sword for that sin alone."

He stared into the distance, still holding her hand. Cass waited.

"Their leader was named Ramos. He was Captain of the Prince's Royal Guard. I thought I knew him. I thought he was my friend." The despair in Thorn's voice was evident.

Cass began crying quietly. Sobbing.

"After… I dropped my royal swords and armor, and when the doors were opened, I walked away. No one stopped me."

He was staring at her hand in his. He was caressing it as if he was trying to memorize it.

"I sold my estate. Always expecting Queen Aleena to send someone to execute me. They never came." He looked up. "I took the gold and found the wife and parents of Ramos. I told them he died with honor and had made arrangements for their welfare. They never knew who I was. Years passed, and the rumors blamed the High Vestal in the great Keep for the plot."

He looked to the window then.

"I was lost. Wandering. I think it's been fifteen years. Leaving death and chaos in my wake wherever I went."

Cass cleared her throat. "Years before the King died, I lived in the capital. I was married to a lesser noble and became lost in the decadence of court life." One of her tears fell on the back of Thorn's hand. "I caught my husband raping a small boy. He gave me these." She gestured to her cheeks. "He sold me to the foulest slaver he could find." She hesitated. "I was never… obedient enough."

Thorn reached up and traced his thumb on her cheek.

"Go find Peck. I need to speak to him."

IV. BUYING CASS

Peck limped into Thorn's room and went straight to the fire and added a log. "Bloody gout," he said.

"Peck, see that black pouch on the mantle? Take it," Thorn said from the bed.

Peck picked it up and looked inside. "Expecting to stay a few years, are we?"

"I am buying Cass from you," Thorn stated. Making clear it was not a request.

Peck froze. Turned his head slowly and looked at him. "You're what?"

"Cass. She's a talented healer; is it enough?"

"Because you terrify me only slightly more than she does, I should tell you… I feel I should tell you," he stammered just as she walked in with another large tray of food.

After a moment, Peck said, as if deciding

something, "Cass, you are free to go as you please. Both of you." He looked at Thorn for a long moment, "For what it's worth, I always thought the King was a bloody bastard and got what he deserved. Thanks again for not burning the inn down, Thorn." He limped out, tossing the pouch of gold in the air and catching it.

"What did he say?" Cass looked at the closing door.

"You are no longer a slave. You're free." Thorn said as she brought him another bowl of soup.

"Free? What does that mean?" she questioned. "Where would I go? Peck tricked you. Now he has me and your gold. I think he freed me long ago. It's why he bought me." Thorn heard her first lie, "To stop my… suffering."

"Why didn't you leave?"

"I did." She brought him a plate of hard boiled eggs, cheese, bread, and an apple. "I went to the Keep to join the order. Become a novice. I managed the thousand steps, but for complicated reasons, I couldn't stay. So I ended up here."

"You've been to the Keep?"

"Yes. And you should not go there." She was somber. "Please, Thorn. The guards are many, and they are cruel. They will never open the Main Gate for you. Never even acknowledge you with anything but arrows."

"You will guide me." He tore off a piece of bread. "To the Novice Gate of a Thousand Steps."

Cass found Thorn out of bed sometime after midnight. The fire had been stoked, and he stood naked before the hearth.

He had her small knife.

She watched him quietly for a few minutes. As she watched, she realized what he was doing.

She slid out of bed and approached in a way to make sure she didn't startle him.

"Give me that, you fool, before you gut yourself." She took the knife from him and began removing the stitches from his chest.

Thorn was amazed at her comfort in her nakedness. He considered who she was.

She was careful and systematic in the removal of the stitches. Chest first, then ribs, and as she knelt before him to remove the stitches in the front of Thorn's thigh, he forced himself to think about the killing of the King. He didn't want to embarrass himself with another reaction.

"What's wrong?" she whispered, as she moved to the back of his thigh.

"Nothing," he said, as he looked at the beams above.

"Your magic flared. I can see it, you know." She continued removing the stitches in the back of his leg and then finally stood to reposition him so she could have better light from the fire to finish his back.

When she was done, she soaked a clean rag in alcohol and cleaned each wound. Magic burned in him again, and by the time she came back around to his shoulder, all the stitchings were healed-over scars.

"Please don't go." She leaned her forehead on the nape of his neck. It was the most intimate moment he had ever experienced. His whole life had been violence and pain and death.

This hurt more than all of it.

"I must go. It is my final task. Live or die. The High Vestal must know the truth. I cannot do otherwise. I am finished hiding from the Queen. I am finished hiding from the truth, only to discover death hides from me."

"They will try to stop you."

"They will try."

She lifted her head from his nape, and he turned to her. They were the same height. Their faces were only inches apart.

His right hand traced the scars on her face. His fingers drifted to the ones on her neck, her collarbone, her sternum.

He recognized this kind of torture. Strips of skin removed, coarse salt or hot irons then applied. He clearly saw now that one of her nipples was missing.

Cass was watching his eyes.

"What are you thinking? Your eyes… are smiling," she asked.

"Forgive me." He looked into her face. "I believe… You're beautiful. Your strength is etched into your flesh. And still, you remain kind. Gentle. I could never be that strong."

"I am anything but beautiful." She choked out the words.

"Beauty seen is in he who sees it," Thorn whispered. "Let us sleep. Tomorrow will be a long day."

Cass wept as he held her. Thorn began to understand why.

Peck was in a joyous mood the next day as the stable boy prepared two of the best horses for their departure. Peck got to keep the other six and all their tack in payment. The horses had no ownership brands, and the tack had no identifying marks, either.

Those men had sought to remain anonymous.

Peck was surprised that Cass was to travel with Thorn. He was also astonished that Thorn would take her. He supplied heavy woolen cloaks as well as clean clothes for the trip. It was only a single day's ride north of the pass to the Novice Gate. North and away from the great East-West Road.

Peck came out to see them off. He stood near the fire at the center of the courtyard. He spoke to Cass first. "I own the stables at the Novice Gate. They will care for your horses. My advice to you is part ways with Thorn at your first chance." He looked at Thorn, "No offense." Back to Cass: "You're always welcome here."

"Thorn. Trust no one. You are swimming in a river of lies and shit. You're not smart enough to keep your mouth shut or to tell the difference. You'll probably be dead this time tomorrow so I'd just like to say goodbye. It's always been interesting."

Thorn reached around and lifted off his personal saddlebags and tossed them heavily to Peck's feet. "If I manage to live, hold this for me. If I'm dead this time, tomorrow give it to Cass."

Cass looked at the bags knowing what they contained. Her hood covered her face as it crumbled in guilt in an effort to hold off tears.

Peck picked the saddlebags up. They were heavy.

Cass whispered to Peck, barely audible as she leaned in the saddle toward him and kissed his head, "Bless you, Kevin." With that, she turned her horse and left the inn to the north on the path behind the stables. Thorn followed close behind.

Thorn looked up to where the Keep should be. Low clouds obscured the mountains. The narrow track led up toward the tree line. He could see traffic from woodcutters that had emerged from the trees before they reached it. The path was clear, and the horses were sure-footed.

V. The Path to the Keep

Their route took them constantly up and north. Paths followed the curve of the peaks and were designed to be traveled in all seasons. There were shelters with unfrozen water along the way, for the horses.

There was little conversation as they finally traveled into the clouds.

It was nearly dusk when they saw large braziers burning to light a bridge that crossed a ravine to a small tower.

There were no guards and the tower entrance stood open, and the road led directly into the mountain through the open Novice Gate.

Cass didn't speak, and Thorn followed her lead. They had to leave the horses in Peck's extensive stable near the mouth of the entry.

They could already hear the murmuring of haunting, chanting, songs from deeper in the mountain.

Thorn breathed it in. Deeply.

There was magic here.

"Do you want to rest or ascend tonight?" Cass asked. "The Keep is only a thousand steps above this place."

"I want to press on." She saw him adjust his swords. The entry tunnel was a natural cave except for the level floor, which was paved in polished flagstone. It meandered about until opening out into a space where they could no longer see the ceiling.

The cavern they were in was vast, with no apparent pillars for support. Clusters of lamps hanging on poles created pools of light that allowed them to navigate. The singing got louder as they drew closer to a large, multi-story stone building.

"The novice candidates are housed here," Cass said, as they looked into the main hall where dinner preparations were being performed by an army of young girls.

"The order only accepts girls?" Thorn asked.

"Yes, for the steps. And women. But not all. Many never even make it to the first step. Some stay and hope they are selected. I was twenty-two when I took the steps, long ago."

Thorn looked at her again closely, beyond the scars and her bright eyes. He wondered how old she was.

"There are usually about three hundred girls waiting. Only one is allowed on the steps each day. Boys enter by the Main Gate. They follow a different path."

"Show me these steps."

Thorn followed Cass around a dimly lit path as the singing got louder. Thorn heard an odd sort of harmony. Some phrases were repeating on different cycles than others. Words blended, preventing him from understanding any but feeling all. There was magic in them.

Before the base of the stairs came into view, a pool of water bordered on the right. It was held in by a thick, head-height wall, so they didn't even see it until they had reached the base of the stairs. It was smooth as glass and reflected the braziers that lined to the path so perfectly it looked like a whole other world inverted.

Every step had a novice standing upon it. Over every novice was a lamp and this lamp illuminated words carved on the wall. They were the words to the song they sang.

Thorn could not read these words or understand the songs.

"The song changes for them after three steps. The two novices above teach the new song to the novice below," Cass said as they watched. "The songs are lessons. It makes them easier to remember."

As the novices sang, each dipped a small pitcher into a basin that was carved into the stone wall and poured the water into the next basin up. Water flowed up into the mountain with the songs.

"Each day they advance a step. It takes almost three years to reach the top," Cass said, as she took off her cloak and an outer layer. There were hundreds of pegs there, but not many cloaks. "We won't need these."

Thorn thought she would be right. With all the people in the stairwell, it would be warm. Add the exertion of climbing the steps for an hour, and they would be sweating before long.

"Why are there no guards?" Thorn asked looking about.

"The guards are up there. These girls represent no threat." She pointed into the stairwell. "Are you sure your wounds are ready for this?" Cass looked concerned again.

"I'm fine." He looked up the stairs tunnel far as he could see before it wound around. There was six feet of space for them behind the novice's backs.

"The first guard will be found with an acolyte in the Chamber of Questions at the top. He will see your weapons… and…" She faded off. "Past that I can show you the way to the High Vestal's chambers. But I do not know how you will pass."

"Leave that to me." He looked at the carved words and listened to the songs. "They will learn these lessons and remember them as songs?" He started up the stairs. "Someone will write a new song about this night."

Cass was hard pressed to keep up with Thorn. He seemed to drift up the stairs. His wide pant legs hid his feet and gave the illusions of floating. Long straight steps gave way to stretches of spiral stairs and sections of an almost raw cave with knee-high steps.

None of the novices gave them so much as a glance. In about twenty minutes, Thorn reached a wide landing where a cavern opened to the side.

Cass got to the landing and caught her breath before speaking. "At the end of the day, the novices from below will rest here."

The stepping basins below fed into a broad pool here, and it supplied the next set of novices.

Thorn cocked his head to each side, and his neck cracked, audible above the singing.

He turned and began the next set of steps.

Thorn waited longer for Cass on the next landing. She leaned over and rested her hands on her knees.

"Did you know that one of the magics instilled in me as a King's protector was the ability to read a person's intent?"

She shook her head no, still out of breath.

"There is evil intent above. I can already feel it." He looked in her eyes. "Peck said to trust no one." He moved closer as if floating. Cass was unable to see his feet. "He knew it was already a foundation belief of mine... I think he was talking about you. Yet you have never really lied to me. But I cannot measure omission."

He didn't wait for a reply. He headed up.

As Cass struggled up the final curve in the steps, Thorn was not in sight. She passed the final novice, went past the last of the dorms and entered an ancient door, the same one the next novice expected to pass through at midnight in a few hours.

A long hallway lined with candle lanterns led to a round high-domed room. The floor was a huge iron grate with intricate mosaic patterns of two-inch square holes with darkness below.

Thorn was there. At his feet was the guard and the female acolyte, both headless. The blood was a stark contrast against her formal vestments.

When Cass was about to speak, Thorn held up a hand and stopped her.

"Tell me only where I need to go."

"Through that door and down a long hall. You will see a large room with two wide staircases, and either one will take you to the vast library down the corridor. The spiral staircase in the great library will take you to the High Vestal's chambers."

"You have done enough. Go back now while you can. They know I'm coming."

With that, Thorn was moving. It was unnerving to watch. The motion he made with his sword sent an arc of blood in a circle, and the sash at his belt wiped the rest as he sheathed his sword. As he walked, his feet could not be seen in his formal black robes. The wide legs of the pants were silent.

He looked as if he was being drawn across ice by an invisible rope around his waist.

Like a ghost, in black, he faded around the next corner. Cass followed, and when she entered the high foyer, only seconds later, she found four more dead guards. One still stood without a head and fell backward slowly like a great tree.

She saw Thorn ascending the staircase on the left. He was so calm and expressionless. She watched the ten guards gather at the mouth of the centered hallway at the intersection.

He stopped and bowed formally to the soldiers. And he waited.

Most of them were nervous and already had their swords drawn. A single soldier, wearing the uniform of the Captain of the guard, stepped forward to face Thorn.

For a long moment, they stood facing each other, three paces apart.

Cass watched, unable to breathe.

With lightning speed, the Captain drew his sword but never got to use it because his torso was bisected diagonally. His sword arm was severed at the shoulder, and his head flew over the railing.

She missed it in the blink of an eye. The heat of the strike's magic rose above his sword now.

Thorn was now standing frozen in a peaceful pose with his sword extended to the right. Blood dripped from its tip. It had all happened in less than an instant.

The other nine men were well trained. In formation, they rushed him.

Thorn danced into the center of them, never stopping at any single point. Heads were dropping to the floor as he went. Cass didn't hear blades cross once.

Only one remained standing. He was six paces behind Thorn. Thorn swirled his sword, and Cass saw the blood arc away again. He slowly turned toward the last remaining guard.

Thorn said something to him, but Cass could not hear his words or the guard's reply. The guard bent over and picked up the sword of one of his fallen comrades.

With a sword in each hand, he advanced quickly. The swords were moving in circles so fast they were invisible, whistling vortexes of death.

Thorn stepped aside, and the guard's leg was severed just below the knee. Before he could fall, Thorn was behind him. A two-handed blow bisected the man's head, neck, and torso all the way to his navel.

He fell forward off Thorn's blade, still in one piece.

By the time she had reached the top of the stairs, Thorn was gone again.

Cass paused over Captain Rankin's body for a moment. She was incredulous.

She gingerly walked around the pool of blood as it spread. It became a waterfall of blood was it slid off the balcony under the rails to the room below.

The long hall was empty. The doors at the end

of the corridor to the library were open. There were ten crossbow bolts stuck into the wooden floor in the opening. Cass was at the door in time to see Thorn running at the wall and leap up. His feet lightly touched bookshelves until he easily reached the balcony above and swung himself over the rail.

The guards there were gathered around the single ornate, black iron, spiral staircase. The guard on that end desperately tried to reload his crossbow. He was run through the heart and was carried along by Thorn, impaled on the sword, around the corner of the balcony and toward the other soldiers.

The dead soldier was bristling with crossbow bolts before they reached the other soldiers that were gathered at the base of the spiral stairs. This group was a mix of spearmen and swordsmen. Some wore heavy armor and some light chain mail. She saw all the spearheads fly off and then men began to drop.

They were all dead moments later.

As Thorn started up the spiral stairs to the next level, he paused and looked down at Cass.

His face momentarily shifted from blank to a

veil of sadness. He nodded and moved on.

When Cass reached the top of the stairs, she could see the two guards outside the High Vestal door were dead, and the beautifully carved doors were broken open.

Beyond the doors she could see Thorn in profile, standing at rest, as if he had just strolled up to the office. Both his swords were sheathed, and his arms were crossed over his chest.

He looked to his right. Directly at Cass.

He was waiting for her.

Out of breath, she slowly entered the room. Looking carefully around the corner, Cass saw a silver-haired woman at the far end of the room, standing behind a grand desk covered with maps and open volumes of all sizes. She was dressed in the formal habit of the High Vestal.

A huge man was standing between Thorn and the desk in the center of the massive, bookshelf lined room.

The silver-haired woman spoke first.

"Cass, I am surprised to see you. When we heard he was here, we were sure you were dead or worse."

She spoke in a tone as if they were in a garden

having tea.

"I hope that…" the silver-haired woman began, but her words were cut off by a rapid clash of steel on steel. The guard had attacked. His first blow had been blocked by Thorn's sword before it was even out of the scabbard. The second strike was deflected by Thorn's second sword.

Both men now had two swords drawn, and they moved in the same ghostly way, circling. Cass could not tell who initiated the next rapid clash. Steel touched steel, deflecting, whirling, the swords moving so fast they were nearly invisible.

The men froze.

They were statues, posed as if to honor the war arts. Moments went by.

"Please, forgive me." Thorn said to the man, twice his size, who moved first.

He was suddenly disassembled. One sword hand and then the other. His right leg at the thigh and then his head was cut in half diagonally between the eyes, across his face--all done before his first severed hand landed on the floor.

Thorn was not even breathing hard.

He visibly relaxed and stood upright at ease.

With his swords still dripping with blood, he turned and walked to the front of the desk.

He cleaned the blood off the swords and laid both on the desk, centered on a large map of the region.

Thorn spoke to the silver-haired woman. She had a line of blood spatter on her regal habit of high office. "On this day, you, ma'am have been the bravest of all."

He smiled at her.

"You may go now," Thorn said and turned his back to her.

VI. The High Vestal

The woman with silver hair fled the room past Cass who now stood in the center looking down at the disassembled man.

"How long have you known I was the High Vestal?" Cass asked Thorn.

"I thought I had my answer at the Elder Bridge. The High Vestal Mother had sent villains to murder me in the darkness." Thorn relaxed more. "I have known since you walked into the room with that tray in Peck's Halfway. You see, I too am well trained in the use of poisons. You had a tray full."

He stared at Cass. His face was blank.

"Why didn't you end me then? Why wait until now?" she asked him.

"End you? I didn't come here to end you. I

came here with a confession for the High Vestal Mother. I did not expect to meet her at Peck's Halfway. Then I thought I'd have my absolution if you murdered me, finally finishing that massacre." He crossed his arms over his chest and leaned back on the desk. "But when you didn't, a new question remained. I could tell all the things you said were the truth. But I also know it is far easier to deceive with the truth."

Cass walked around the desk and sat in the great chair. "Ask then."

"Why did you want the King dead?"

"Because he was evil. The world is far better without him." She looked him in the eyes. "I'll not change my answer to avoid your vengeance. Even if it costs my life, the world is better."

Thorn let out a great sigh.

"Your men failed." Thorn paused. "Ramos was their best swordsman and was my equal. He killed four of my brothers. He was severely wounded. Brother Saris and I dispatched the rest and eventually restrained him before my King.

"The King said to him, 'You have fought well, my son. Tell me your name and your family so that I can send you home to them with honor.' And

Ramos told him." Thorn could not meet her eyes. "And when he was done the King laughed. Instead of a quick, honorable death, the King stabbed him in the stomach, spilling his bile and his intestines. A slow death for man as strong as Ramos."

Thorn briefly closed his eyes, remembering.

"While Ramos lay slowly dying, the King told him how he was going to send troops to his home to rape, torture and burn his family at the stake along with their whole village."

Cass's hand went to her mouth.

"Saris and the King began to laugh… So, I killed them. Saris first."

She stared at Thorn in shock.

"I killed the King."

There was a long pause as Thorn watched the pieces of the puzzle align in her eyes.

"I brought Ramos a merciful death after I told him that his family would be safe and cared for. He died with honor. He knew his goal had been achieved."

Cass paced the room and finally stood, the desk between them.

Thorn continued, "When you came to me at

Peck's Halfway, I thought you didn't want my chaos and violence brought to the Keep. The High Vestal Mother would know what I could do. Know I could not be stopped, even wounded."

Cass was thinking, her brow heavily creased.

"When you brought me to the Keep I knew why."

"Why?" She asked.

"These were not bodyguards, they were jailers," he said. "You used me to kill them. They did not belong here. I could feel it. You were in exile a mere day's ride away." He closed his eyes again. "I never knew Peck could be so brave."

Her chin trembled. "I knew what you did for Ramos. But not why. You could not have found his parents without speaking to him," she said. "The Queen… she was…"

"When they finally broke the door of the Cathedral down I was alone. I was surrounded by the dead. I was drenched in blood. The room covered in frost." His eyes were still closed. "I kept expecting someone to stop me, to strike me down. They never did. They let me just walk away. The curse, it seemed, was to live."

She finished her circuit around the desk and

now stood between Thorn and his swords. Slowly she moved closer to him.

He studied her face. The scar in her right eyebrow, the worry lines of her eyes, the flecks of gold in the brown of her iris.

She turned back to the desk and lifted the short sword. She stood face to face with Thorn, grasped his red sash, and cleaned his sword again in one slow motion. She looked at the blade and marveled at its beauty. She studied the grain of the steel, and its balance in her hand before sliding it into its sheath. He had grown still as a statue. She repeated the cleaning with the long sword.

She paused this time to study the staghorn handle, its natural polish, and beauty. She slowly slid it home.

"Are you injured?"

"Not much," he said, as he began to relax finally. "Are there any others that you require I kill this day?"

"There is a garrison above with just over three hundred men, not including the boys." She looked at the man on the floor. "But there are only three more of these." She locked eyes with him again. "You've already ruined my favorite rug." A corner of her mouth rose.

"Oops." His eyes flashed his smile.

VII. THE QUEEN OF LIES

"It was the new Queen all along," Thorn said, as Cass searched her library, hurrying. "I now believe she seduced King Reddick, murdered his wife, and later his only heir." He held his hand out to stop her searching for emphasis. "Then she manipulated you to use your influence to kill the King." She drew away from him as if he burned her.

"And then she stole from me all that I had," Cass fumed. "I was not in the Keep when it fell. By the time I got to Peck's they had held the Keep."

"Not for much longer," Thorn said.

Cass showed Thorn maps of the keep.

"The main hall here is several levels up from

where we are." He pointed to the corridor on the same level as the upper Keep. "The barracks are here. The Main Gate is here and the officer's quarters are here."

"One of the guardians is always on duty here, in the watchtower. The top is enclosed in glass, and the fire burns there continuously. It can be seen for miles," Cass said. "The level just below is the…" she hesitated, "the portal room."

Thorn nodded his understanding. Cass was relieved she did not have to explain the significance of it to him.

"Is it a circular room with thirty-two doors? How many doors are unlocked? Do you know where they go?"

Cass brought out another map. It showed a beautifully rendered ink drawing of the Keep, including the Watchtower.

"This makes sense now. How many portals from the tower access the Keep? There are usually at least two." He was studying the map. It had the interior of the two levels of the Watchtower. One was windowless and had thirty-two doors depicted. Only six were marked.

"These two. One goes to the tower at the Main

Gate, and one comes to this office." Cass pointed to a block of cells on another map. "But there is a third portal. It goes to a different circular room. It's how they got in at the beginning. That path has not been used for hundreds of years."

"The doors locked from the other side are lost to us." She shivered and looked at him. She could see her breath. "Are you all right?" She noticed a cut in his tunic.

"I'm fine." He pointed to the portal room and one of the marked doors. "Where does this one go?"

Cass sighed and straightened her spine, making a decision. She walked from behind her massive desk and over to the built-in bookcase beside the large fireplace. The shelves were covered with various relics instead of books.

She reached up and pressed a spot on the end of the mantle and pushed the shelf inward at the same time. It swung in.

"They didn't know about this one." She took a candle in with her and lit an oil lamp on a shelf.

It was more like a short hallway six yards deep and three wide. The opposite end had a simple, rectangle door frame, carved with runes in deep relief. The dark wood timbers that made the frame were a foot thick on a side. The door was the same dark wood, bound with black iron. The hinges were on the left, always on the left.

"You've seen these before?" Cass asked.

"Yes. I have used them many times. There is a bridge room, a portal room, in the capital. I have seen two others."

"I have only used this one portal. From here to the Watchtower and to the Main Gate. The ancient sorcerers that created the network of portals left us no clue how to open them." She hugged herself thinking what was on the other side. "We can't wait long. The word may spread quickly."

Thorn nodded. He was ready.

Cass reached up and retrieved a key from its hiding place on top of the carved frame. Thorn shook his head as she unlocked the door. She handed the key to Thorn and pulled on the great ring.

There was a stone wall on the other side.

Cass stared. "They locked the other side. How?"

"The Queen. Thorn pushed the door closed

and looked at the frame. With his left hand, he reached inside the slit in his tunic and brought out bloody fingers. He began to paint the black relief areas around a particular rune. After a half a dozen applications the rune was entirely surrounded by his blood.

It began to glow with a faint light from within the grain of the wood.

Thorn twisted the rune.

He pulled the thick iron ring and revealed another door where the wall was moments ago. "Beyond this door is another hall the same size as this?"

Cass nodded, still speechless.

"Stay here until I come back for you," Thorn said as he pushed open the other door.

Thorn disappeared into the darkness beyond the door.

She stared into the darkness and saw the far door open into the circular portal room. That door swung into the chamber as well.

Thorn moved silently to the right and

disappeared from her line of sight. The far door remained open and showed the thick column in the center with the open spiral staircase that wound around it. The torches all burned between each door. Thirty-two doors. Thirty-two torches. Always burning with Earth magic that even she didn't understand.

When she saw Thorn begin to ascend the stairs around the column, she moved forward. She gently, quietly, closed the door behind her as she entered. She knew it wouldn't lock.

The room was warmer, and all she could hear was the flutter of the torch flames.

Then there were voices, calm and strong, but she could not understand what they were saying.

Cass started up the spiral stairs. The column was thick, and the stairs were narrow and went one and a half times around the stone cylinder as she approached the opening in the domed ceiling.

They were still talking.

Cass carefully looked over the edge of the floor to see both men standing in the bright light of the round chamber. Thorn was standing casually relaxed, with his swords in his sheaths. She had noticed that posture before. She knew it was a trap, ready to spring.

The Guardian was naked to the waist and soaked in sweat. He had been practicing sword forms. His sweaty long black hair was dripping wet in a pony-tail. His large, double-edged, two-handed broad sword was pointed at Thorn.

"Do you miss the touch of a true blade, Thorn?" He taunted, "The soft feel of it as it stands up in your hands? It's the difference between the fine daughter of nobles and a pock-faced farm girl."

In a blaze of speed, the Guardian attacked. The sword that had been pointing at Thorn an instant ago was arcing around to come down in a devastating downward cut that would have been impossible to deflect with all the power in it.

Except Thorn was no longer there.

Cass had not seen Thorn move in close and pass just to the Guardian's side. She had not seen him draw or strike.

The Guardian's sword struck the floor as his momentum made him fall forward in two bloody pieces, completely cleaved just below the ribcage.

Thorn was like a frozen statue for a heartbeat.

The Guardian tried to drag himself across the floor for a few seconds before death found him. Thorn's eyes were watching Cass, as she ascended into the room.

The room had the single column in the center that rose twenty-five feet where the flame began and rose another twenty feet above that. The wall around the room was twelve feet high. The glass dome was above that wall.

This room was hot. The cold air was being drawn up from the level below with the vented chimney effect from the massive flame.

She looked at the body. "Two down. Two to go?"

"Yes. But the others will not be so easy. I have met them. They are the Queen's Guardians. The best and most vicious of them." Thorn cleaned and sheathed his sword.

"What will we do next?" Cass asked.

"We wait here. The changing of the watch is within the hour. With luck, they will come to me one at a time, here."

VIII. Sharkey

They had to wait just ten minutes.

Cass had ascended the single narrow stairs. They were barely stairs, more like rocks that were mortared to protrude a foot out from the wall. She walked around the top of the wall to the other side where the guardian would see her as well as the body. They hoped the distraction would be long enough. Thorn would be behind the column as he entered.

As he appeared casually coming up the steps, he said, "Hello, Thorn." He didn't seem to notice the dead guardian or Cass at all. "Word has come up from the lower levels of your visit." The huge defender had full chain mail and heavy ornate, lobster-like, articulating plates on his chest, back, and shoulders. There was already a double-bladed ax in one hand and a double-edged sword in the other.

"Hello, Sharkey." Thorn used his nickname from his youth, knowing he hated it. "Been keeping yourself busy, I hear, killing the weak, and being the Queen's whore."

Thorn could see one of those insults hit the mark.

"Did Arnor and Viktor die well?" Sharkey asked as he topped the stairs. He was still thirty feet away, not looking at Thorn.

"They have been training. I was impressed." Thorn lied. "I didn't think Viktor could get any taller, but he seems to have managed."

"Yes…" Sharkey moved with incredible speed, throwing the ax at Thorn in a deadly horizontal spinning flight, "…he has."

Thorn barely had time to draw his short sword and deflect the ax from ripping into his chest. Sharkey crossed the distance and was swinging a double hand overhead blow with blinding speed. Thorn's left hand was numb from the impact with the ax. When his automatic defense of the next death blow reacted with both swords, it was too much. While the swing was deflected, Thorn lost the grip on the short sword. It spun away toward the wall.

Neither was speaking now. The fire roared above as they circled each other. Their sword tips pointed at each other's hearts, but their swords were a foot apart. They stopped rotating with Sharkey between Thorn and his short sword.

They stood still for a few moments before Sharkey spoke. "I heard you carried farmer blades, but I had no idea they were kitchen wives fish knives."

"Fish knives for Sharkey," Thorn said and attacked. A dozen strikes were parried with the same speed they were delivered. The ringing steel was impossibly loud. Thorn retreated in an attempt to draw him away from his short sword.

It didn't work.

Sharkey never looked away from Thorn as he hooked his toe under the blade, flipped it up to his left hand and threw it at Cass where she stood on the wall. She barely dodged it, but it struck the glass point first and shattered the foot square pane of glass, passing into the darkness beyond.

"That was your only chance, Thorn." Sharkey

smiled. "You don't have the reach, strength or stamina to take me now. You rely too much on your draw tricks and surprise."

Without a word, Thorn advanced and avoided Sharkey's swing instead of meeting or deflecting it. Instantly he was inside Sharkey's guard, inside his arms, spinning to face away, his back to Sharkey's front.

Thorn's sword did not slash. Its point entered Sharkey just below his chest plate and moved upward through his guts, his stomach, his heart and then protruded out just to the left of his neck.

Thorn released his sword, leaving it inside the man. All four of their hands now firmly held the grip of Sharkey's sword. Thorn need only let death take hold.

Sharkey released the sword and clamped his iron hands on Thorn's neck. Thorn dropped it and was trying to pry his fingers off.

Then Cass was there.

She had rushed down, and instead of helping Thorn pry at fingers she grabbed the handle of Thorn's sword and began to twist and wrench it savagely side to side. A great gout of blood burst from Sharkey's mouth, and he fell backward.

The sword slid out of him as he fell.

Thorn was having trouble breathing. He also had a large wound from his hip to his knee. He choked out. "Help me. Up there." He gestured with his chin to the stairs to the top of the wall. They were so narrow she could not help him up.

Standing below, holding his bloody sword she watched him reach the top and turn to the massive flame. His arms extended out, and his chin rose.

The glass behind Thorn began to frost. The great roaring jet of flame leaned toward him.

The room was becoming cold.

Thorn let out a scream of agony as he absorbed the power. It looked like his body was full of magma, glowing in his screaming mouth and the cracks of his wounds, as they began to close.

The gashes healed and the bruises disappeared as his scream faded.

The flame returned to normal. The frost on the glass melted from its heat.

Thorn collapsed to his knees.

Thorn never lost consciousness, but it was close.

He was about to fall over when Cass was by his side, holding his face in both hands.

His focus returned as he exhaled a breath he did not know he was holding.

"Thorn, say something. What did you do?" Cass pleaded.

He looked into her eyes.

"I don't suppose you happen to have any food with you?" he said in a hoarse voice, as he smiled and began to stagger to his feet.

He looked down at himself. His clothes were bloody rags.

Cass handed him his sword, and he automatically cleaned it and slid it into the scabbard. He drew the short scabbard out and dropped it. He adjusted his clothes and tightened his belt.

"The last one will be Torrock," Thorn said. "Even fully healed I may not be able to overcome him. Sharkey and the others were always too proud, too certain of their prowess. Not Torrock. He is the most cautious and brutal of all."

"What will you do?" Cass was checking his flesh. Wounds that had been there were wholly gone.

"When Sharkey does not return with my head, he will come here," Thorn said.

"Hello?" a voice called from the stairwell below. "My lord, Thorn… sir?" It was the voice of a boy. They proceeded down as he was emerging from below.

"I'm here, lad. Stay where you are. You don't need to see this," Thorn said, as he reached the same level.

"That is the best sight I've seen in weeks, sir." The boy was surveying the two dead bodies. "Your day's not done yet, I hate to say. Master Torrock sent me to tell you he awaits you."

"Where is he?" Cass asked.

"He is standing in the inner courtyard. Waiting."

"What's your name, son?" Thorn asked.

"My name is Penn, sir."

"Lead the way, Penn." Thorn gestured. "You don't happen to have any food do you?"

IX. Torrock

The portal they took accessed a room in the guard tower at the Main Gate. It was a brilliant placement for strategic reasons. An impossible number of men could flow out of that portal to operate the gate to the surprise of any intruders there.

When Thorn went from the tower to the battlements, he could see Torrock standing alone below. He was in brightly polished, full plate armor, head to toe. He held a large torch aloft as he waited. On seeing Thorn emerge, he turned and entered the keep via massive double doors.

Penn ran down the steps that went from the battlements to the courtyard and followed the receding torchlight through the open doors.

When Thorn entered the main hall, the light was

receding down a corridor at the other end. They continued to follow the light as it moved through the keep, down stairs, through feast halls, armories, and eventually into a long wide corridor with cells on either side. Torrock had placed the torch on the wall in its place and waited. Two swords were drawn. They were medium length. He was still as a statue.

The helmet he wore had only a slit in front for vision.

"I remember sparring with you, Torrock. Even blindfolded." Thorn spoke low and even casually as if they were having lunch. "You disdained armor as much as I did." Thorn entered the pool of light, his sword was already drawn and raised over his head. He drifted across the floor in an eerie motion.

Torrock didn't move.

"I will allow you to divest the armor unmolested. Then we shall see what kind of swordsman you have become." Thorn paused out of range. The guttering sound of the torch was all the sound there was.

Torrock's armor bristled with sharp blades. His

shoulders, forearms, biceps, elbows, and knees all had fixed, shining knives as part of the bright, horrible beauty of his armor. Torrock remained silent.

"Have you become so ugly you cannot even reveal your face?" Thorn's attempts to anger him might as well have landed on deaf ears. Thorn began to slowly circle him to the right when he could see past Torrock into the open cell beyond.

There was an open portal arch in there on the back wall.

"She wants to speak with you…" Before Torrock could finish his sentence, Thorn struck. There was a blur of strikes, counterstrikes parries, and hits to armor, when suddenly, as fast as it started, Thorn's blade was shattered by opposing strikes between Torrock's swords and Thorn's left bicep was impaled on a forearm blade.

Thorn screamed but never stopped moving.

He tore his bicep clean through as he spun and stabbed the remaining twelve inches of his sword into Torrock's eye slit.

Torrock fell like an avalanche of blades. His helmet wrenched the sword handle from Thorn's grip. He used his right hand to hold his left arm together.

He turned toward Cass; Penn was still by her side. "Stay here. Penn, make sure she doesn't follow me." The corridor was getting cold.

As Thorn passed, he pulled the remains of his sword from Torrock's helm. He moved directly into the portal.

X. ONCE DAMNED

Thorn passed through the door into another round room of closed doors. Sunlight shone down the spiral stair in the center. He ascended into a warm, opulent suite. The architecture and daylight was completely different. There was a large living area full of rich carpets, lounges, and piles of pillows. Decadent was the only word in his mind. Every wall was floor-to-ceiling windows that looked out on a tropical beach on one side and lush jungle on the other.

Trailing blood as he went, he carefully moved through a dining room, a library, and a bedroom with an enormous finely carved bed. Beyond this, he found the Queen.

Aleena was in a bath chamber. She relaxed in a

pool up to her chin in water. A fire blazed in the hearth nearby.

"I don't like to be kept waiting," she pouted as Thorn stood in the doorway. He leaned on the frame so he would not fall. "Why did you bother to bring that? You won't be able to use it. Not after what you did to my poor husband."

Thorn could already feel the compulsion to drop the sword. He focused on the pain and stood straight. Thorn stepped forward. The closer he came, the more he knew he would be unable to bring the steel to her flesh, the spell was so strong.

He began to feel something else.

Queen Aleena rose up out of the water to stand with her arms along the edge of the pool, her breasts now exposed, barely out of the water. Thorn could see runic symbols tattooed on her skin, her breasts, and the undersides of her arms.

He was becoming aroused.

"Yes. Thorn the damned. I am going to take you as you bleed. Again and again. Take sex from you as you scream. Because you will not be able to stop me. Now bring that pot of hot water here to warm my pool."

He focused on the pain. He went to the pot

heating over the fire. He had paused before he upended it, extinguishing the blaze.

"I like defiance. I took the King, I took his son, I took all the Royal Guardians," she gloated.

He stepped to the edge of the pool.

"I dominated them all, just as I will you. Because it is only worth the trouble if they are lions…"

He stepped into the water, onto the first stair, ankle deep. Through gritted teeth, he spoke.

"Once Damned. Always Damned."

He drove the broken blade into his own leg, just above the knee and ripped an enormous wound straight up through his thigh to his hip. This was followed by several lightning stabs into his other thigh.

The Queen was laughing.

He carved three slashes down his chest and finally stabbed the shattered blade deep into his own heart.

The Queen laughed at his decision. "Suicide over seduction?" she laughed as the broken blade finally fell to the floor.

As Thorn's arms came up, his back arched, and his mouth opened in a scream.

The water instantly froze, trapping her. His wounds began to glow as if lava were about to spill out. Frost covered the room as he screamed the endless stream of agony and despair. The queen started to panic and tried to rise, but it was too late; she ceased moving. A light frost crept up her flesh. Her mouth was frozen open in a silent gasp. Her eyes glazed white.

Thorn was a silent statue now as well. Arms held wide as the inner glow began to fade before the wounds had closed.

Drawn by his howl, Cass burst into the room. The room was so cold, clouds of her breath instantly crystallized and fell like snow. Grasping the scene, she rushed to the fireplace. It was a block of ice. She grabbed the huge iron poker. It was so cold it burned her hands. Moving across the room at a run, she swung with both hands and shattered the queen's head into tiny pieces. Her frozen jaw remained grotesquely attached to the stump of her neck.

Cass kept moving until she reached her true goal. She swung and shattered the window.

"Quickly! Break the glass!" she yelled at Penn. Moving along the wall, she broke window after floor-to-ceiling window. Penn went the opposite way, using a bronze statue, grabbed along the way. "All of them!"

The tropical breeze flowed in from the seaside. An icy fog flowed out the other side.

Thorn was glowing inside again.

Thorn awoke, crawling back from oblivion slowly, his mind empty. His eyes fluttered open and were presented with a warm, rich scene. Dark oak beams that covered the ceiling were illuminated by a roaring fire in a beautiful hearth. The tapestries on the walls depicted a horse race over a lovely countryside of fields, rolling hills, and hedges to jump.

As he turned his head, he noticed that on each of the four walls the race traversed four seasons as well. When he turned toward the winter scenes, his gaze fell on a pale-skinned shoulder. A scarred shoulder.

He carefully moved to face her back. His left arm wrapped around her as the memories washed over him. The realization that his severed bicep was healed was his only fleeting thought of the past as he kissed the nape of her neck. The past and the future were lost in the scent of her, the warmth of her.

She started as she became aware.

She turned quickly to look into his eyes. She touched his face as if to make sure he was real. "Are you all right…" was all she could choke out before tears began to flow.

He kissed her mouth in answer. The salt of her tears was the best thing he had ever tasted.

"I took you to the Watchtower." She was having difficulty talking past the lump in her throat. "You soaked the magic in for nine days. It was the wound to your heart that took the longest to heal." She buried her face in his neck. "I was so afraid. Then, yesterday, you sighed and seemed just to be sleeping again. We brought you to my quarters in the keep."

Over her shoulder, he could see the recovered two staghorn handles of his swords. Both blades were broken, but the handles were intact.

This made Thorn smile.

"Are the portals secure? The portal rooms?"

"Yes. Thanks to you." She said to his neck.

"The Capital is in chaos, the High Houses all vying for the Throne."

"Do you happen to have any food?"

She laughed, and it was like music.

Justice in the Mist

I. Ruins

Ash sat in the overgrown ruins of a pilgrim's shrine, oiling his ax as the rain fell. He was not the first to camp under the large, slate roof. Massive carved wooden pillars held up the moss-covered shelter. The pillars were so thick his arms couldn't reach around them. The abandoned shrine was open on three sides, but the forest was so dense that there was no wind. The fire was his only light, but it illuminated the entire space. His horse

Crocket and mule Bastion cropped grass at the edges of the shelter. Ash recognized the carvings but could not read them. He was surprised the influence of the Vestal Tower had reached this far north. His axe held similar runes. He could smell the magic on the ten columns.

The vine-covered statue of a meditating monk had long ago lost its bald head, which now rested across from him like a silent host staring into the fire.

Who were you, so loved that they built this shrine for you?

Quill, his wolfhound, was hunting in the rain. Ash set down his axe and stirred the pot that hung over the fire. It had wild onions and taters in it with salt and spices, awaiting its final ingredient, whatever it might be.

Ash finished oiling the ax. The oil briefly highlighted the runes engraved there. It was a simple woodsman's ax that never needed sharpening. He easily shaved a section of hair from his arm with the edge. He could have cleaved the stone monk's head in half with it, and it would still be razor sharp. Instead, Ash would use it to replace the firewood he had found cut and stacked there by the last traveler. He liked that common practice. It indicated the type of travelers that passed this way. But it had also been a long while since anyone else had used this shelter. The wood was very dry. The forest had reclaimed what had once been a road that went by this shrine.

Ash sat cross-legged on his horse's blanket. He rested the butt end of the ax on the ground like a wizard's staff as he watched the fire.

The rain brought a hush to the forest beyond the firelight. Despite the rain, Ash heard a crashing movement through the forest in the stillness. Closer than he liked. He strained to hear the familiar sound of Quill's loping gate. The lazy wolfhound would chase his prey to the camp, so he didn't have to drag it so far after killing it.

But this time, the sound was different. As the hound entered the firelight, Ash realized something was chasing Quill.

Quill was not moving fast this time, so Ash didn't get up.

The massive hound bounded into camp and dropped a big groundhog he had in his jaws. Following him, a small boy skidded into camp and spun around when he saw Ash. The boy faced out into the forest, then backed up until he was against the stone back wall of the ruin.

A man slowly came into the light with his sword drawn. He said nothing at first as he took in the situation. He had been chasing the boy, and the boy had followed Quill. The wolfhound had led them both to Ash. Quill stopped panting and bared his teeth silently between the man and the boy.

Ash met the child's eyes for just an instant. They communicated all he needed to know. Ash didn't move. The hound moved beside the lad, who placed a hand on Quill's shoulder, never looking away from the intruder. The terrified boy could touch the antisocial animal, even with its teeth bared and hackles up.

"It's a good night to be out of the rain and enjoy a bowl of stew," Ash said as the man advanced out of the rain and approached the fire pit.

"I'll enjoy some stew after my business is done here," the man said as he shook the rain from his hair.

Ash raised an eyebrow. "Put up the sword. There's a tale or two worth telling here. What kind of business? A good place to start."

"The kind one can't have witnesses…."

"Don't." That was all Ash got out before the man swung a killing blow of the sword at Ash's neck.

A look of surprise froze on the man's face when his blade was blocked, embedded in the handle of the woodsman's ax. The muscles in Ash's arm were like they were cut from stone. He looked into the man's face and tilted his head as if the man had just asked a stupid question.

The instant the man forced his blade to escape, Ash moved like lightning and was on his feet in an instant.

The man's head split down the center, and the ax didn't stop until it wedged in the middle of his sternum. The ax was the only thing holding the man up. A single push sent the dead man out into the darkness and rain.

"Are you all right, lad?" Ash held the ax in the deluge from the eaves to rinse off the blood and gore. "Quill, see if there are more." The hound leapt into the night.

The boy was frozen where he stood. His eyes were wide with shock and horror as he stared at the blood rinsing from the ax, a normal reaction for those unaccustomed to violence.

"Are you all right, lad?" Ash repeated gently as the boy bent over and vomited in the rain. It took him a minute to compose himself enough to reply.

"I am now, sir." The boy was wiping his mouth on his wet sleeve.

"Are there more?" Ash examined the damage to his handle.

"I don't think so."

Ash nodded and sat back down to clean and skin the groundhog expertly. When it was quartered, it went into the large stew pot.

"What's your name, son? What's this all about? I didn't expect to see a single person in this forest." Ash started cleaning his knife and gestured for the boy to sit.

"My name's Lin. Lin Tanner. I live just outside the village of Llangollen." He was finding it difficult to speak.

"This isn't a good place to be lost. This forest isn't kind to strangers," Ash said.

"Yes. No. Kinda. I was searching for a lost girl." The boy shuddered. "I've never been this far south."

"Searching for who?" Ash picked up his ax and examined the damage. A black iron, rune-covered rod in the center of the handle was exposed just below the ax head. He retrieved a saddlebag, took out a long strip of leather, and began wrapping the damaged part of the handle as a temporary measure.

"I was searching for Iris Glover. Everyone is. They all think she's dead." He hesitated. "I kind of got lost."

"If you plan to wander, be better prepared next time." Ash added, "And what about him? Did he kill the girl, Iris?" He pointed to where the body was in the darkness. "Did you know him?"

"He stopped me on the South road and asked about our village. And the blacksmith, Hale. But he didn't know his name. And after I gave him directions, he immediately tried to kill me. He chased me in the rain through sunset and wouldn't give up. Then I saw your dog with the groundhog in its mouth in a clearing, watching me. He had a collar on. I knew he was with someone. Someone else." Lin sat close to the fire, on the monk's head.

"When the rain started, I couldn't believe he didn't catch me." He fell into silence. They sat that way for a long while. Finally, Ash began fishing out the bones from the pot as the stew simmered.

Quill returned with his fur soaked from the rain. He paused by the fire long enough to get a nod from Ash and walked to the far opposite end of the ruin. With his nose facing the fire, he gave a massive shake. Water soaked that end of the shelter, but none reached Ash or Lin. Quill returned to the fire and settled there to dry one side, then the other.

"In the morning, I'll see you home before moving on my way," Ash said. He was examining the ax handle again. "Maybe you can point me to this blacksmith. I think I need a new handle."

They each had two large bowls of stew. The large pot was still half full and sat cooling on a flat rock. Ash said quietly, "Quill. It's all yours." The hound got up and began to eat directly from the pot. "Quill has come to enjoy his food cooked. He brings me all the game now. He likes roasted meat from a spit better than stew, though."

When the pot was empty, Ash slid it under the eave so the rain would fill it for Quill.

"You killed that man," the boy said. "I saw it and still can't… believe it."

"That man placed no value on life. Not even his own," Ash said to the boy sincerely. "He would be alive now with a belly full of stew had he made different choices." Ash paused. "Now get some rest. We'll leave after first light. The rain will likely be passed by then."

II. MORNING

Ash woke with the dawn. The fire was already stoked and warm. The calm air and shelter held the heat close. The old-growth forest was soaked and shrouded in fog. Ash had slept deeply, all the way through the night, knowing Quill was on guard.

"Do you always sleep sitting up with that ax in your lap?" Lin asked after Ash lowered his hood.

"Not always." Ash reached over and retrieved a bag from the pack. "Sometimes I sleep in the saddle." He smiled and tossed the boy two large apples.

"Your horse and mule wandered off," the boy said, while chewing. "They're in the clearing back there eating autumn clover."

"Quill will bring them back when it's time." Ash stood and stretched.

"Is it all right if I keep some of his things? I don't have a good knife." Lin pointed at a small pile of personal items by the fire. There was a knife, belt, pouches, the sword, and water skin. "Or is it theft?"

Ash looked at the items. There were no identifying markings on any of them.

"Keep them. Do you see how plain they are?" Ash took the sword and plain scabbard and tucked it into the pack-mule's load. "This was a bad man. He was intentionally hiding who he was. Have you ever seen things like these that weren't personalized?"

They dragged the body to the other side of the shrine and buried him beneath a cairn of collapsed foundation stones.

Ash saddled his horse, Crocket, first, then Bastion, rearranging things a bit so Lin could ride the mule with the supplies. It didn't take long, and they were on their way.

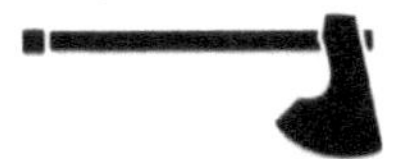

"You called this the South Road? Not much of a road. More like a deer track," Ash said.

"They say it used to be a road decades ago," the boy said. "Look at the trees along here. Not through them, up." He pointed ahead. "The big ones to either side. The village elders say they are glad no one but ghosts use the road anymore."

"Why do they say that?"

"They say the woods are full of the raiders' ghosts and children that got lost," Lin said. "I think they tell stories to keep us out of the woods."

"You don't believe in ghosts?" Ash was amused.

"Oh, I do. I see them in the mist sometimes," Lin said. "I'm just not afraid of them. Nothing to fear, really. When the King was murdered, they say, chaos came like a storm. Garrisons that kept peace on the roads to the south were withdrawn to the capital. There were raiders, and Tregaron wolves came down from the mountains. Harsh winters, poor harvests, sickness. The grandelders love to talk about it. So many died then. The ghosts haunt them. It was all before I was born."

Ash could see through the mist. Massive trees flanked a lane of saplings where the road had been several decades ago. He could smell the magic in the mist. It was subtle. There was irrational fear in it. Fear of getting lost forever. Fear of… impending doom.

"Does this fog ever lift?" Ash asked.

Lin looked about as if noticing it for the first time. "I guess," he replied absently.

They passed two farm ruins along the way. They were burned-out cottages and barns, now abandoned and overgrown. When the forest undergrowth began to thin, the fog's dense mist began burning off, and Ash could smell chimney smoke as it approached midday.

"This is our farm," the boy said, even though there was nothing to see yet except overgrown fallow fields, a stream, and pastures surrounded by rotted and fallen, split-rail fences. Massive tall trees competed for light far up into the sky.

There were signs of tree harvesting long ago, but the remaining trees were simply too big to harvest now. Also, there was no windfall here—a sure sign of a human settlement nearby.

As they rounded a bend, a clear road appeared ahead that showed evidence of repeat wagon traffic. Eventually, in a clearing on the left, was the small farmhouse.

III. The Stone Farm

It was just a tiny stone farmhouse with a deep porch that wrapped the entire building. There was also a barn with steep roofs of cedar shingles. A fenced orchard paddock had goats and an old mare. The barn had sheds filled with cords of firewood. The clearing sloped down to a pond. Ash could tell after a few minutes that Lin's farm was a shadow of its former size. But what remained was well maintained.

A woman was exiting a chicken coop holding an apron that Ash guessed was full of eggs. Lin waved as two dogs began to bark.

Lin looked down, and Ash's hound was terrifying at full height, hackles up, head down and teeth bared. "Quill, they're friends," Ash said casually. At Ash's words, he relaxed. His tail began to wag rapidly, and his tongue hung out the side of his mouth. Then, he bounded forward to meet the dogs that welcomed him like an old friend to sniffs all around. Soon they were off bounding through the fields together.

By the time they reached the farmhouse, the woman had delivered the eggs to the kitchen and stood on the wrap-around porch with her hands on her hips. She was trying to act angry, but the relief in her eyes was stronger.

In an over-obvious attempt to deflect, Lin introduced Ash. "Mother, this is my new friend, Ash. Ash, this is my mother, Holly Tanner."

Ash bowed from the saddle, never breaking eye contact. The same gesture he would have afforded to a noble. Lin easily slid off the mule and ran to hug his mother around the waist.

"I'm sorry, Mother. I'm fine, thanks to Ash. I'm just fine." The boy was trying not to cry then.

"You were gone two nights. Without your pack. You know how worried I was." She looked back up at Ash. "Thank you, sir. There seems to be a story here. I have soup and fresh bread. Can I persuade you to have a meal, with my thanks?"

Ash slid down from the horse, and both Crocket and Bastion stepped up to a rain trough and helped themselves.

"Thank you. That would be most welcome. You have a beautiful farm," Ash said casually so Lin could collect himself.

"Yes. We're fortunate in that regard." She patted the boy and said, "Take Ash and show him where he can clean up. I'll see you inside." She turned and entered the house.

Ash made no move to remove the saddles or load from his animals. Instead, they began to graze on the lush grasses as Lin took Ash around the porch, where a shelf was attached to the wall and held a pitcher of water, a bowl, and some towels. He washed his hands and face, and when Lin was done, he refilled the pitcher.

Beyond the garden, the hounds chased butterflies together in the field. It was an idyllic scene. Yet it made Ash uneasy as he took off his cloak and hung it on a peg. He felt like he was being watched. The scent of the mist was gone from the air, but not his mind.

The cottage was a single-room house with a half loft. The space was dominated by a central fireplace that was both functional for cooking and structural for the building. All the heavy beams above went from the thick stone walls all around to the chimney pillar. The beams carried single lines of runes—the same as the shrine in the forest—so darkened with age that you'd not notice them without looking for them. The stone of the walls and hearth was cut so precisely no mortar was visible. The mass of the stones would keep the house warm on long winter nights. An integrated bread oven was pure luxury in a house this small. The loft above was Lin's domain. He was up a ladder instantly, ignoring the stairs, and back, wearing clean clothes in a flash. Below the loft was a bedroom with a wardrobe and two overstuffed chairs. The open side had a long table with a bench on each side and fine chairs at the ends.

The floor was planks. He had expected a packed earthen floor with threshing. The planks were even waxed. Ash was now self-conscious about his boots. Luckily, they weren't muddy.

"Please sit," Lin invited him as he rushed about bringing bread and butter and honey. Plates, bowls, utensils, and a pitcher of cider, one of water and another of milk. He even brought cheese, apples, and fruit Ash didn't recognize.

Holly swung the pot from the cook fire and ladled servings into bowls Lin brought to the table. As Ash's eyes adjusted to the dim indoor light, he noticed the frames around the front and back doors were made of stone, beautifully carved to look like wood.

"I got lost again, Mother," the boy told her casually as he held the first bowl. "Ash saved me from a bandit. He tried to kill us, but Ash killed him first."

Lin was oblivious to Holly's reaction. Ash watched her closely from across the table. Ash slow blinked and nodded his acknowledgment of Lin's words.

"Even though he tried to murder us, we gave him an honorable burial in trade," said Lin. "So his spirit can rest. So his ghost can move on." Then, self-consciously Lin added, "I finally have a good knife, and this is for you." He poured out a leather pouch full of gold and silver coins.

"Have you been talking to Osgar again about ghosts?" Holly said as she looked at Ash with a raised eyebrow.

"I was settled for the night, sheltered out of the rain, when Lin came running into camp seeking sanctuary. My fire and my hound had drawn him. Hot on his heels was a man chasing him with a sword drawn, determined to end the boy. He tried to kill me straightaway." Ash paused. "He failed." Ash dipped a piece of bread into his soup and took a large bite.

"I was searching for Iris and met the man," Lin said. "I gave him directions to Llangollen, like that man a few years ago." He explained faster and faster. "He asked after the blacksmith. He didn't even know his name. And then he just tried to kill me. I ran. Fast! He kept chasing me. Quill found me and led me to Ash in the rain." Lin stopped himself from spinning up anymore.

"And what of you, Ash," Holly asked. "What're you looking for in the great forest?"

"I was moving south before the snows. I have a home there where I spend the winter trapping." Ash tore another piece of bread and dipped it into the delicious soup. "I may have to visit this blacksmith to repair my woodsman's ax. It was damaged in the attack."

"The only strangers I ever see are men like you," she said. "All of them to see the blacksmith."

"Men like me?" Ash asked. "Trackers, you mean?"

"No. Not just trackers, but all drawn here." She raised a skeptical eyebrow. "The shadows grow long already, and it's an hour's ride to the village. It has no real inn anymore, just a tavern. I can offer you the barn for the night."

"That's more than generous," Ash said sincerely.

"Lin, go out and see to the horses, please," Holly said to him, but her eyes never left Ash.

"Yes, Mother." And he was gone at a run to appease her.

"Don't take the Tregaron wolf with you when you go into town. Had I not seen the collar, I would have never believed it," she said after her son was gone.

"You've seen one before? Few have."

"Twelve years ago, just after Lin was born, a single pack killed half the men in the village, including Lin's father. Lin doesn't know the details. That after the worst raids in years. We almost starved that winter. The wolves ate or drove off almost all the livestock and game in the region before moving on. They say they must have killed all the raiders as well. Thus the ghost stories." She looked out a window. "I've never seen a Tregaron collared."

"I didn't think packs came this far out of the mountains."

"They did that winter." Holly looked into the fire, remembering. "Somehow… they even got into the inn. The pack got in and killed everyone inside. They dragged the bodies off. The inn burned down, with half the village in chaos. Our town blacksmith was the first to die. He met the onslaught with a hammer in each hand. Lin's father was the last to die, saving us here."

Ash let her speak. She was looking around her own house as she remembered.

"That spring, we almost left." She looked back at Ash. "And then he arrived. Hale, the new blacksmith. Without a word, he just moved into the old blacksmith's place. And started working. Rebuilding. He was improving everything. He always seemed to know what to do next. Never leading, just doing. Everything turned around."

"I hope he can fix my ax."

"You remind me of him," she said. "Why are you really here? Are you looking for Iris Glover?"

"I'm looking for someone, but it's not Iris. It's what I do. I find people. For people," Ash said, holding eye contact with her.

"With a Tregaron wolf?" she said. "Llangollen is a town of mostly good people. Families. There are no heads worth taking here."

"I'm only delivering a message if I find who I'm looking for. I'm not a bounty hunter. Just a simple tracker."

"Who are you looking for?" she asked.

"I have no idea who they are, only what. A sorcerer…" Ash chuckled as he said it.

Holly barked a laugh and was embarrassed by a snort that made her laugh more. "You'll find no wizards here. Only hard-working farmers and woodsmen."

That is not what my nose tells me. Then the voice whispered in Ash's mind unbidden, *Iris is dead, murdered.*

"In three days is the Autumn Festival. The harvest is complete. The season's mast trees are cut already, dried, and made into rafts on the Cardiff River. Then, after the festival, a dozen of the men will deliver the mast logs to the coastal shipyards."

"How do they get back?" Ash asked. "That's a good distance."

"With the proceeds, they buy two or three wagons and animals to bring them. They buy seeds and salt and other goods we can't make ourselves. New livestock to keep our herds strong. They're usually home before Solstice." There was pride in her voice. Then she looked at the pouch of coins on the table. She slid it to him. "Thanks for protecting my son. He's all I have."

Ash slid the pouch back.

"I don't need it. I already have more coins than I will ever need. Lin was courageous. It's his. He earned it," Ash said. "Buy me a new ax handle, and we'll be even."

"Deal," she said with a nod, and Lin rushed in.

"Quill has a deer for you," Lin said. "My dogs, Patches and Wicket, are really excited."

Ash rolled his eyes.

"What's wrong?" Holly asked.

"Quill is trained never to accept food from anyone but me. He only likes cooked meat now." Ash sighed. "He'll catch it, but I have to cook it."

Holly had a musical laugh. "Lin, bring the haunches and tenderloins in here. The cook fire is nice and hot. Leave the rest at the edge of the field for Patches and Wicket. They're not particular."

Holly had an extra-large pot simmering by the time Ash and Lin were back with the meat.

"Just boiled is fine. He's a spoiled brat." Ash looked over, and Quill was at the open door. "Quill, check the perimeter."

Holly watched the hound nod and head off.

IV. THE BARN

The tack room in the barn had a cot that gave Ash a good night's sleep. The barn was well-made with a sound roof. At breakfast, it was decided Crocket and Bastion would stay at the farm with Quill while Ash walked into town with Lin. Holly needed a few things from the village before the festival and sent a list along with her son.

They had a mountain of scrambled eggs with gravy, biscuits, and venison for breakfast. There were gallons and gallons of maple syrup, butter, and honey in the pantry. Lin was proud of it all. He managed the beehives, milked the goats, and collected maple sap when it ran in the spring. The village came together every spring and ran the sugar shack. Lin ran off to do his morning chores before leaving for the village.

Sipping hot cider, Ash sat back from his plate. Holly watched Lin as she buttered a piece of biscuit, added honey, and sat back to drink her tea.

"Your farm seems to be doing well," Ash observed. "Do you have livestock besides goats?"

"Since my husband died, it's been more challenging. I can't handle cows like we used to. But we've managed somehow. The garden overproduces enough to feed a few pigs. The hedges are all kinds of berries. The trellises are covered in grapes," she said, looking out again. "Lin loves it here. We have orchards with apples, peaches, pears, and some nuts. The goats graze beneath. The days are long. We produce and harvest far more honey and maple syrup than the village needs. We have goat's milk and make butter and cheese—and there are so many eggs. We also do ciders. We trade our surplus in the village for whatever we need." Holly sighed. "Our neighbors bring a deer to us now and then to trade for honey."

She knows they are still only one harsh winter away from starving.

Ash thought of the mist that seemed to linger in the forest at the edge of the farmlands. "No more trouble with wolves… or people?" he asked carefully over the top of his mug of cider.

"No wolves. We don't get many people here. Most can't seem to find it unless you've been here before." Holly said it like she was glad for it, but there was something else in her tone. "We aren't on the way to anywhere. The road once had more traffic when there was a town on the Cardiff River. I think the town was called Castlerock long ago. It's gone now, burned by raiders. It's only foundations and ruins, but the bulwarks and docksides are all stone and still there. It's where we launch our mast trees."

Lin ran in, skidding to a stop. It was almost comical how he waited to speak until spoken to.

"Are you ready to go?" Holly asked with a smile.

"Yes, ma'am." He beamed. "Cart's ready to go."

"Thank you for breakfast," Ash said as he stood.

"I'll keep him out of trouble," Lin pronounced as Ash put on his small backpack.

Lin had a small cart pulled by a well-trained large goat named Danny. It was nibbling the grass beside the path. The small cart was full. It had two bushels of apples, a basket of eggs, and several jars and jugs.

They walked a while without seeing anyone else or even any other farms. Lin's dogs were leading the way. Quill was nowhere to be seen.

When the village chimney smoke could be seen, farms appeared on both sides of the road. The road was now more than a path and had noticeable wagon traffic. The forest was farther away beyond pastures and fields.

Lin and his goat must have been a common sight on the way to town. People waved. Happy dogs ran out for an ear scratch.

V. The Village

"There's the Mill Bridge." Lin pointed as the village came into full view. A mill wheel slowly turned in the autumn sun. A narrow creek powered the wheel. The blacksmith was on the other side of the street from the mill, just beyond the bridge. The doors of the forge were wide, and the ringing anvil's sound sang into the air.

"I'll visit the blacksmith and maybe others for a bit. After that, I can find my way back." Ash said to Lin after they crossed the bridge. Ash noticed the bridge, the mill wheel, and the road all faintly smelled of magic.

"After I'm done here, when I get home, I was going to go fishing and mush-rooming," Lin said. "Can I take Quill with me? Dinner is just before sunset."

"Yes, you may if he's there. He'll probably be out hunting," Ash said as they entered the blacksmith's.

"Hale! This is my friend Ash. He needs his ax fixed. 'Cause a man tried to kill me, and Ash stopped him. So I'm to pay whatever it costs, Ma said. Here are the knife and sword he had. I'm keeping the knife. Can you sharpen it for me? Ma said I could. I guess Ash keeps the sword. Ma said no to that." Lin spoke in a rush to the smith, who stood at the anvil with his back to them. He froze between strikes but didn't turn to them. Instead, he held up the horseshoe with tongs he was pounding and examined it. Then, after a moment, he quenched it in a water barrel and tossed it into a bin with other shoes. He set the tongs and hammer down on the anvil. Only then did he turn to lock eyes with Ash.

Ash's only ability was to sense magic. That was why he had been given this task. He could see that the blacksmith's anvil glowed with magic. But the man himself seemed to be utterly devoid of it, unlike other sorcerers Ash had met.

Lin placed the knife, sword, a small basket with a dozen eggs, and a single gold coin to pay for the new ax handle on the smith's bench. He didn't see the fierce look on Hale's face. He waved as he ran off to complete his rounds.

Without a word, Hale held out his hand for the ax.

I have found my sorcerer.

Ash had unwrapped the handle on the walk into the village. He placed it, almost ceremonially, into the blacksmith's hands. The blacksmith began to examine it closely, handle first. Then, he raised an eyebrow when he saw the runes engraved into the ax head.

"Where did you get this ax?" Hale asked.

"It was a gift from a friend," Ash said, lying with the truth.

"Do you know what these poll-runes mean?" Hale asked.

"Yes. Do you?" Ash replied.

Hale replied with a raised eyebrow that brought wrinkles out on his forehead all the way to his bald head.

"Is what the boy said true? Because in an hour, the entire village will hear a version of it." Hale easily twisted and snapped the ax handle off its neck. Next, he slid the wood off the carved rod that ran down the center of the handle. The rod was also covered in runes. Then, holding the ax head, he tapped the butt of the steel rod on the anvil until the broken remains of the handle slid out from the ax head.

"It's true. Except my hound saved the boy." Ash looked over his shoulder in the direction Lin had gone. "I let the boy keep the man's knife. It would help if you examined it and the sword. You can keep the sword. You will find no maker's marks. An assassin's blade. I think he may have been coming here for you. He was asking after you."

"You picked a poor day to wander into this village," Hale said. "Bringing stories of murderers in the woods. The baker's eldest daughter is missing." Hale looked closer at the extracted rod. "I will have a new handle for your ax by this time tomorrow. You may need it."

"What do you mean by that?"

"I've known several of the King's Trackers. They wander the land knowing a humble woodsman's ax is but a tool, not a weapon. Everyone needs to chop wood. So they can carry their ax, even in cities where weapons are prohibited. The staghorn knife at their belt is another humble farmer's tool. Beside a fork and spoon, it's mundane, for hunting and eating, not stopping a man's heart."

Ash slid his staghorn knife from its sheath and handed it to Hale.

"Did she give this to you as well?"

"She?" Ash smiled.

"I made this for Cass, the High Vestal of the Tower," Hale said as he blew a breath onto the blade. Ash's vision saw magic runes alight—ones he had never seen before.

"So it is you. She sent me to find you. Almost a year ago. But you were gone, without a trace. So I kept looking," Ash said as he took off his pack. He opened it and began digging.

"How did you find me? I thought I had been careful. You must be very good."

"I heard rumors of a haunted forest and village that was impossible to find. I can sense magic when it's close enough. Like the faint smell of smoke or a chill in the air. It took me almost a year."

A young man entered the smithy. He was just out of his teens and heavily muscled. He was shirtless except for a thick leather apron and wore a leather skull cap to keep the sweat from his eyes.

"Ash, this is Alden Green, my apprentice," Hale said as he wiped the sweat from his bald head. "Alden seems to have lost his shirt again."

"Skin washes easier than my shirts," Alden said as he bowed briefly. "If the story is true about you saving Lin, don't be surprised if the council wants to speak to you."

Ash could smell desperate fear in this boy. Fear that was barely held in check.

Fear is magic that all people carry, echoed in Ash's mind.

"Why would that be?" Ash replied.

I already know why. I want you to tell me.

"Iris Glover is missing. Three nights in a row," Alden said, and fear spiked from his words. "And she ain't Lin. He'd wander a week out there and not notice he was lost, and his Ma'd not blink an eye." Alden was hesitant. "I'm… worried about Iris. It's not like her. Not at all." Alden returned to carrying in more iron bars from outside before saying more. It was clear he was upset.

This boy… young man, is full of pain and fear. Of what? Iris?

Ash had produced a cloth bundle the length and thickness of his forearm. He unrolled it on the counter. "She wants to know if you can fix these. For him. She said you'd know who."

The bundle contained the pieces of two shattered swords. The two handles were simple staghorn, but the artistry was exquisite.

"So Thorn is not dead yet?" Hale asked as he studied the ruined blades.

"No such luck for him. Yet," Ash replied as if expecting the question. "He continues to try."

"Thorn was the last man to find me before I came here. And he was lost then. Damned and knowing it. I felt him use his doom as a weapon."

Ash nodded, knowing the whole story. "He guards the tower now."

"Have you been to the high tower?" Hale asked.

"Yes. It's a cold place surrounded by snow and… mist. There is too much magic there…too loud or bright for me. I can't sleep there," Ash said. "I don't like it much. But they still hold true to honor there. That's enough for me. The turmoil around the palace regarding who will next sit on the throne keeps me away from the capital. A

King's Tracker without a King is not… valued by the highborn of the capital. So I was easily forgotten."

"The King's Trackers were always a closely held secret," Hale said. "Powerful in their abilities, training, and humble ability to go anywhere."

Hale rolled the bundle back up and looked Ash in the eye. "I'll have your ax handle ready tomorrow. When you return, bring the hound but leave him under the bridge. You may have need for him." Hale glanced out the open doors. "I'll talk to them tonight. By tomorrow none of them will think you took her. And I know the value of a King's Tracker."

VI. QUILL

Ash left the smithy but didn't go into town.
Instead, he took the path under the bridge, where
mist was hanging. Quietly he said, "Quill. Come."
The hound had been shadowing Ash.

The path skirted the village. Slowly Ash
explored as the sun rose to noon. The land was
higher on the village side of the path, and on the
other side, the trees had been cleared for fields of
grain, corn, and other crops. In rainy years, the low
plain on that side would flood. It made the soil
rich.

No one saw him pass in the mist. No one saw
Quill quietly catch up to Ash, either.

"Find anything?" Ash said as he watched the
runes on Quill's collar glow with his words,
allowing Quill to understand them perfectly.

Quill shook his head no.

There was another bridge on the far end of the village. Adjacent to the bridge was the tavern. Ash could hear heated discussions. It was about him and Iris. He could also hear dogs barking.

Ash looked at Quill.

"Call them down here," Ash whispered.

Quill waited until there was a pause in the barking, and he let out a single "Woof!"

A few moments later, Patches and Wicket bounded down the embankment and through the tall grass to find Quill hiding there. Lin was close behind. He fell backward in his tracks when Quill stood. The hound was taller than the boy.

"Lin, I want you to do me a favor. Please tell your mother that I will not be back in time for dinner. But I will be back tonight, closer to midnight. I'll be quiet."

"What are you doing?" Lin asked as he munched a luncheon meat pie.

Ash stood to full height before continuing. "I heard about Iris. Quill is good about finding people. Like he found you. We're going to look for her."

"I can help. I'll come along!" Lin was excited.

"You've given your mother enough gray hair recently. So take your dogs, Danny, and the cart home with the things she wanted for the festival. Remember: tell her where I went, but don't tell anyone else. No one except her."

Deflated, he said, "Yes, sir."

"And Lin, tell her you didn't want her to be alone, with strangers about," Ash added. "She'll like that."

Lin smiled at the sound of that. "I looked for you at the smithy. Hale liked my new knife. He even said so, which means it's true 'cause he don't talk much. When he does, he means it. He sharpened it!" Lin proudly turned his hip so that Ash could see. "He even stamped my name on the sheath. See?"

His name was stamped there. But there were other decorative runes as well. Lin's knife would now never blemish or rust. It would stay sharp longer and be next to impossible to misplace.

"Be safe, Lin," Ash said. Quill huffed a short, not-quite bark, and Patches and Wicket heeled perfectly to either side of the boy as he made his way back through the grass.

Ash knelt by Quill and ran his fingers over the runes on the hound's collar while scratching his ears. Then, whispering the words the arcane High Vestal had taught him, he felt the animal quiet. Ash didn't remember closing his eyes, but Quill stared into them without blinking when he opened them.

"Go, boy. Find her…." At those words, Quill bolted away into the mist.

Ash explored the village, unseen for the rest of the afternoon. He used stealth, not magic. All the while could sense the general direction Quill had gone like a sound he followed in the distance, but the sound was in his mind.

After the sunset, Ash crossed the North Bridge unobserved in the darkness. He paused at the top of the arch.

Ash had had this feeling before.

Something had happened here… or would soon.

He marched north in the moonlight on the road, following the distant howls of the Tregaron wolf. There were no farms on this side of the village, only moonlight in the mist he breathed.

Trees stood vigil on either side of the road like silent pillars.

Less than an hour later, Ash left the road. Two stone's throws into the forest, the rafters of a ruined cottage rose into the moonlight like the ribs of a rotting carcass. He was close enough now to hear the whine rising from Quill, where he sat waiting for Ash.

Between them was a low rock circle, a well. Its opening seemed frozen in a scream. The shadows from the trees gave it jagged teeth. The mist lingered a few hundred paces away on the far side of a clearing.

Ash looked down into the gaping maw. He needed no magic to smell death in there.

When Ash and Quill quietly approached the farm, it was late, and the harvest moon was almost full and high in the sky. Quill silently alerted Ash to her sitting on the porch swing in the dark. He waved Quill on and he instantly became a panting, loud-breathing hound that could be heard easily as he approached instead of the silent predator he was. Noisily he climbed the wood steps. His nails clicked on the wood as he approached and licked the offered hand before plopping down at her feet.

"Everything, all right, Holly?" He could see her silhouette in the moonlight. She reached over to the porch rail and retrieved a bottle. She refilled her cup and then held up another in a silent offer to Ash. "Please." It was almost a whisper in the night.

"Lin told me about Iris today," she said and took another sip. Ash joined her as he sat on a log used as a stool. "Osgar questioned him for an hour because he went missing when she did. So Osgar has decided the man you killed must have murdered Iris. Or you did. Strangers rarely find Llangollen."

"Tell me about Osgar?" he asked as Quill heaved a sigh.

"Osgar Langson. He's somehow head of the town council. He's the closest thing we have to a mayor. He's the most superstitious man I know, but he's good with money and finds the best buys and pricing for our masts. But, as a person, well, be your own judge. He didn't believe Lin, not even about you, until Alden spoke up about seeing you today."

"He's worried like the rest. Even Alden is worried," Ash reassured her.

"Osgar had them search where Lin said he had been. They found the grave, confirming part of his story. They even saw what you did to the man. They came right by here." She paused and took another drink before continuing. "They said I'm to bring Lin to the village tomorrow."

She wasn't crying, but Ash could tell she was on the verge.

"I had a good talk with Hale today. He's speaking with Osgar and the council tonight. So we'll sort it out," Ash said.

"Iris reminded me of myself, Ash. More and more. She is…was as tall as me already, same color hair minus a few grays. I've got a horrible feeling. Osgar will only make it worse. He's so full of himself."

"All Lin said about him was that he badly needs a bath," Ash said light-heartedly.

Holly laughed. It was music in the cool air. Ash saw tears finally tumble onto her cheeks in the moonlight. He found himself wanting to brush them away.

"Lin's a good lad. They know him," Ash soothed. "What bothers you so?"

"It's the man in the woods. And you. And the mist," she said.

"What about the mist?"

"You never would have found this place. The mist somehow stops them. It does not stop as much as it diverts them subtly. The only way here is to be brought by someone from here… or to follow them here."

She knows about the mist.

"That man was following Lin, not chasing him." Ash sipped the strong drink. "It was lucky Lin was lost just then. Lin, being who he is, would have shown him the way. Instead, he needed a way in to get to… Hale."

Ash risked reaching out, stopping most of the way. She took his hand, and they sat in a long unbroken silence.

"I know Hale is a sorcerer. I feel it most out here on the edge. Even with Lin, I couldn't do all this myself, the prosperity, the protection in the mist," she said. "I remember the starving days before he arrived."

"I know a bit about magic. A sorcerer can't make all this happen." He gestured to the farm. "All they can do is help allow it to happen. All the rest is the magic you bring."

"Can Hale find Iris?" she thought for a moment. "Or will he simply allow for her to be found?"

Ash took a deep breath and exhaled through his nose. Quill raised his head at the sound. He squeezed her hand gently.

"Holly, I believe Iris was murdered. I need your help to prove it."

VII. The Tavern

The entire town was milling about outside the North Bridge Tavern when they walked into town the following day.

Lin and Ash were walking, and Holly rode Crocket, Ash's horse. Lin walked with his hand on Quill's neck. Lin's dogs jumped and played with Quill as they went, and Quill had his goofy, smiling face on with his enormous tongue hanging out to one side.

In front of the tavern, Holly dismounted.

"Quill, tell the boys to stay out here and guard the horse," Ash said, and Quill made the strange huffing sounds again, and Lin's dogs lay down by Crocket's hooves. "Lin, follow me with Quill, just like we talked about."

There was a stage at the far end of the large common room, typically used by musicians or storytellers. There was a table there now with three people sitting behind it. Lin spoke first as they entered the small open area before the table. Islands of people deep in discussion fell silent and moved out of the path of the Tregaron wolf. Two shepherd hounds with broad chests and long snouts raised their heads to Quill momentarily but lay back down unperturbed.

"Quill, lie down, buddy," Lin said, and Quill immediately flopped down comedically in a well-practiced trick to be disarming and cute. While Ash looked back at the amused crowd, he noticed Hale leaning against the wall. He seemed disinterested.

"Llangollen Council, this is Ash, the woodsman that saved my son two nights ago," Holly said. "Ash, this is Erma Greene, Lane Burch, and Osgar Langson."

Before Ash could return a greeting, he was interrupted by Erma Greene. "How dare you bring that thing in here? Do you know nothing of what happened in this village, in this very room!"

"Quill is a good boy, a happy boy. Aren't you, buddy?" Lin said as he scratched Quill's belly and got his face licked.

"I can assure you that Quill is quite well-behaved. Whose dogs are these? They agree." The two shepherds had raised their heads when Quill entered but remained calm and didn't even get up.

"Enough!" Osgar barked from the center of the table. "What's your business in Llangollen?"

"I heard from young Tanner here that there was a blacksmith here that could fix my ax," Ash said. "The lad spoke true, thankfully. But I also understand that a girl is missing. I may be able to assist."

The crowd was silent, but almost in unison, they subtly glanced at the blacksmith, who nodded.

"Why should we trust you when it's more likely that you killed her than any of us?" Osgar said, well aware of the insult.

"Killed her? We know for a fact that she's been killed?" Ash said. "I assume that she's just lost in these vast woods. Even an experienced wanderer like young Lin Tanner here can get lost now and again. And we're wasting time. All I need is a piece of clothing Iris wore, and we'll be off. If she's out there, I'll find her. It's what we do." There was a commotion in the room as someone ran to the baker's home for the clothing.

"Why should we trust you?" Erma Greene asked. "Let's say you and your wolf find the girl's body. Wouldn't it be just as likely for you to find her because *you* killed her?" Her tone was polite.

Ash liked her. It was an excellent question.

"Hale has my weapons, even my bow, for repairs, sharpening, and general maintenance. My gear, goods, and all my worldly possessions are at the Tanner farm, except my hound and horse. So send riders with us," Ash said.

"Why would he be here at all if he had done anything to Iris? He would have run. I say let him try," Lane Burch added.

"I'll go!" a voice shouted out as Alden, the blacksmith apprentice, pushed through the crowd.

Fear and…guilt? Still rose from him like steam…

More than one person looked at Alden suspiciously. Including the council.

"By your leave. If anyone wants to help search, we'll ride as soon as the runner returns. Quill, come, boy," Ash said, turning on his heel. He exited with the conversation rising in his wake. Quill was by his side as he mounted Crocket.

Ash felt a hand on his thigh. Holly looked up at him. He liked her hair in a ponytail. It allowed him to see her whole face. His heart skipped a beat as he sensed another magic from her eyes, her words.

"You be careful," she said.

"You be careful as well." Ash laid his hand on hers.

VIII. Tracking

Seven men and one woman were mounted and ready to go a few minutes later, including Osgar and Alden. Osgar was squinting suspiciously at Alden. Then, finally, a young girl came up to the side of his saddle. "This is Iris's nightgown. Will this work?"

"Thank you, miss. This will be perfect." When Ash moved Crocket ahead and said, "Quill, up," Quill stood on his hind legs and placed a paw to either side of Ash on the saddle. Their heads were even, revealing the true size of the Tregaron wolf.

"What do you expect that beast to do?" Osgar asked from his saddle. Skepticism dripped from Osgar's voice as fear steamed from his shoulders.

"I expect him to find her." Ash was holding the nightgown so that Quill could have a good sniff.

Quill dropped down and began sniffing in the packed earth, almost running in random circles. The people on horseback began to follow him as he moved to the south Mill Bridge.

"Wait. He doesn't have the scent yet. He'll signal when he does," Ash said as they waited in uncomfortable silence in their saddles.

"It's unfortunate that you killed the man who could have led us to the body," said the one woman in the group. Her face was profoundly wrinkled, but she sat proudly in her saddle. Quill let out a howl as if on queue and made a beeline toward the North Bridge.

"Where does this road go?" Ash asked. Osgar was on one side, and Alden on the other.

"It goes to the river, nowhere. That's a half day's ride," Osgar complained.

"Why would she go this way?" Alden asked.

After only twenty minutes, with the trees to either side already closing in on the road, Quill was a hundred paces ahead of them, barely visible in the mist, but suddenly stopped at the right side of the road. They were only a mile outside the village. When they caught up, Quill plunged into the forest. He moved at a slower pace now.

"This is absurd. Iris was fifteen, almost sixteen years old, and she'd never get lost this close to the village," someone said.

Pines and fog obscured the views in this section of the forest. They briefly lost sight of Quill but saw him at a complete stop when they rounded some pines. He was on the far side of a cottage ruin. The foundation and stone chimney stood. Bare rafters pointed to the sky. Quill stood over a low wall circle.

It was a well.

Alden lost control and revealed what he had been hiding poorly—his feelings for her. "Iris!" he shouted, as he dove from his saddle. "I'm here!" He was at the edge of the well. "I'm climbing down."

"Wait. Let me get this rope on you." Ash dismounted, carrying a heavy rope that he secured around Alden's waist.

"Don't be absurd. The stupid beast is probably just thirsty and smelling water," Osgar scoffed. "No hound could track any scent after the rain we've had!"

Ash wasn't the only one looking sideways at Osgar now. His mount was nervous as well.

In no time, Alden's voice echoed up. "I'm at the waterline. The water is freezing."

"Does anyone have a lantern?" someone asked. No one did.

"I'm going in. I have to know." They could hear the plunge into the water and the gasp from Alden. People began to dismount.

"It's only waist deep. She's not here." Ash was watching Osgar's face. Then Alden added, "I found something. I'm coming up." As Alden was climbing, Quill was circling the well, sniffing.

"It looks like a sleeve," someone said, holding it up as Quill hungrily sniffed it.

Quill began circling the ground around the well and the riders. He stooped suddenly for a moment and then loped off with his nose to the ground.

"Quill has a second scent, another trail he'd like us to follow." Despite being wet and cold, Alden handed Ash a pale blue piece of cloth before he took to his saddle.

Osgar went from red-faced to pale. "This is a waste of time," he said, before turning and heading off. Two of the other riders followed him.

Another howl sounded when he had a scent.

Quill was moving much slower on this trail. He followed it back the way they came. It took them another thirty minutes to return to the North Bridge at a walking pace. They could see a crowd gathered in front of the tavern. But Quill left the road just after the bridge and descended to the path under the bridge. He followed that path as it wound around. A set of narrow wooden stairs climbed the abutment, then the back wall of the tavern to a closed door on the second floor.

"That's the back door to Osgar's rooms," one of the riders said.

"Quill, come down." The hound descended the stairs and then sat looking up at Ash. He sat in his saddle, thinking. "Quill. Go now. Seek. Find her. Bring her back," Ash said, and the hound ran off down the path and around the bend.

The four riders sat in a circle for a few minutes without speaking.

Ash turned Crocket to return to what was happening in the village. The four riders stayed on their mounts at the back of the crowd as Osgar ranted from the balcony above.

"And here he is now. We had no problems in this village until this man arrived. And for what?

To see the blacksmith. Hale is the only reason I've seen strangers ever come to this village. And for what? Shoes for their horses? Repairs to pots and pans? NO! Weapons. Killing tools…"

Osgar froze mid-rant, eyes drawn down the village lane, far past the gathered crowd.

The crowd turned as one.

In the distance, through the mist, Quill strolled toward them beside a barefoot girl in a muddy, pale blue dress that was missing the left sleeve. Her long brown hair was damp and disheveled. Only one eye was visible through the tangle of hair. Her face was dirty. She glanced to her left as she passed the bakery. Iris's parents stood on the porch holding each other, sobbing.

She stopped a dozen paces behind the riders. Her sleeveless arm slowly raised to point at Osgar. People were now flooding silently onto the balcony behind Osgar.

She damned him with the silence.

"The hound led us back to Osgar's back door," one rider said to the crowd.

"A blind cat could track the smell," another said.

"I found her sleeve in the well," Alden shouted above the crowd as he held it up, then fell to his knees.

This broke the silence in Osgar.

"She's a lying whore," he ranted. "A witch. In league with that blacksmith demon and that outsider with the Tregaron wolf. Do you not remember them, what they did to us? She's a witch. They're devils and sorcerers! I knew it. I killed you, strangled you. Threw your lifeless body headfirst into that well to *protect* this village! She's a *witch*, back from the dead!"

When Ash spoke, everyone could hear him, even though he didn't raise his voice. "When you raped her repeatedly, was that also protecting the village?"

"That proved she was a witch. She never once cried out!" Osgar was now clearly insane. He was unaware that several hard men were now holding his arms as he screamed.

The girl raised her hand and scratched Quill's ear. Then, she combed the hair back from her face with her left hand.

It was Holly Tanner.

IX. The Stone Bridge

The next day Osgar was to be hung from the North Bridge. Ash was surprised no one else from the village was in attendance.

When he demanded his last words and the sack was removed from his head, Osgar discovered only the last two members of the council stood witness from the river path below. Ash and Hale held his arms in iron grips as he perched on the bridge rail with the noose on his neck.

"You finally got my seat on the council. You never had the courage to kill me yourself. I knew it." Osgar spat in Hale's face.

"I'll never take a council seat. Yours or anyone. Now or ever," Hale said quietly, so that only Osgar and Ash could hear. "I could have killed you with a thought whenever I wanted if I ever gave you a second thought. But you were right about one thing. I am a sorcerer."

Hale's eyes glowed red for an instant. Horror filled Osgar's face. He turned to the two witnesses below and tried to shout a warning. He had no voice. They released his arms, and he stood with his hands tied behind his back. Osgar balanced on the bridge rail on his own, frozen in terror. Osgar looked back at Hale, mouth open in a silent scream. He toppled off the bridge as if of his own volition, and the rope snapped his neck.

The two council members turned and moved along the path.

Walking away from the bridge, Hale asked, "You found her in the well that first day we spoke. Didn't you?"

"Yes. Finding people is what we do—Quill and me. Dead ones are the easiest. Unfortunately."

"How?" Hale asked as they walked. "Osgar was right about the rain."

"Quill is trained to find dead bodies. It's not hard. It's the smell. Tregaron wolves can smell the rot of a corpse a mile away. Additionally, most people, especially women, are murdered by someone they know," Ash said. "People are stupid and vain, especially murderers. And lazy. They don't want to carry bodies too far. Too much risk of being seen. After the fact, the other council members noticed Osgar was directing the search everywhere except there."

"What did you do with the body?"

"That very night, I returned her immediately to her parents. They begged me to find out who did it. Her mother had never seen that dress before." Ash looked toward the baker's house as they passed. "Cleaning her up made it clear she'd been tied up, raped, and strangled with a rope. They promised to remain silent until it was over. They let me take the dress. Even though it had spent a day in the cold water of that well, it still wreaked of Osgar. Who knows how many times he used her."

"How did Holly get involved?"

"I told her everything when I got back that night. I was an outsider that had no real evidence. An outsider that 'knew' where the body was. I knew how that looked. And Quill scented the trail back to Oscar's door that night. Holly knew Osgar well, knew how he would spin and deflect," Ash said. "In the end, it was Lin's idea. He somehow knew Osgar had nightmares about ghosts."

"I had heard those whispers as well," the blacksmith said.

"I think the man I killed was coming to Llangollen to kill you," Ash said. "Can't know for sure."

"Not the first time," Hale said as they entered the smithy. "The forest is full of their bones. The justice in the mist usually handles them. Lin was in the wrong place at the right time to find you. I feel the hand of The High Vestal at work."

Hale reached below the counter and brought out the ax. He handed it to Ash. It was almost ceremonial.

"Is this Ironwood?" The new handle was a mat black and beautifully shaped and smoothed. On either side of the neck were engraved runes.

"This handle will never break. With the runic rod within and on the outside… these runes will make it, let's say, more useful." Hale touched the runes gently. "If you've more leather, wrap the grip to make it seem more like a simple woodsman's ax."

He retrieved a cloth bundle and laid it out on the counter. Opening it revealed the two swords made whole. They were held in two new humble leather sheaths. The staghorn grips gleamed with fresh polish.

"How? There was barely enough time to fix my ax handle."

"I knew, I sensed, the moment the swords were broken. Their purpose was fulfilled. I began these on the same day two years ago. They simply awaited the grips to return."

"Thank you. The High Vestal said you would refuse payment. I see in your eyes already that it's true."

"And what of you, Ash?" Hale said. "What of your magic?"

"I've no magic of my own. I merely use magical things that I see. I don't need to understand how they work to use them. Like this ax, Quill's collar, and other things."

"That's what they all think. The Seeing is a kind of magic," Hale said. "If that's the case, I've one more thing for you.… and Lin."

X. Goodbyes

Ash walked to the Tanner farm and watched Quill play with Patches and Wicket in the pasture where Bastion and Crocket grazed nearby. There was no sign of Lin or Holly as Ash saddled up his horse and mule. When he was ready, he went in search of his hosts.

Stepping onto the back porch, he saw a pile of satchels for the mule: supplies prepared for the road.

Knocking as he entered, he found Lin stirring a pot of stew. Glancing over, he saw the table was set for just two.

"Leaving, I expect," Lin said, not looking at Ash. "Ax all fixed, and you're gone then?" Ash heard the catch in Lin's throat.

"Before I go, I wanted you to have some things." Ash held up a leather case. Lin looked over. "I know you'll continue to wander. These will help keep you safe."

The boy came over as Ash opened the case revealing two brass tubes, each an inch in diameter and six inches long. "Each of these is magic. Keep them secret."

Ash lifted the first tube. One of the end caps had a cleverly designed latch and a spring-operated hinge. When he opened it, there was a spark and a flame, like a candle. "I know a lad as smart as you can start a fire easily with flint and steel, but magic may be better in an emergency. Or in the rain." Ash handed it to the boy. "Some magics anyone can use because it was made by a sorcerer."

Lin opened it, and the flame was still there.

"Use it sparingly. This magic won't last forever."

"What does that one do?" Lin pointed to the other tube. It was slightly different.

"This one is extraordinary." Ash lifted it and walked to the back door. "Sorcerers forged and polished the magic crystals that are contained within." Ash lifted and extended the spyglass to three times its length. "It will bring distant items closer. Give you the eye of an eagle. But you must be very careful with this one as the magic is fragile as well as powerful and will never fade if you care for it properly. Here, try." Ash placed a lanyard attached to the tube around Lin's neck.

When he brought it to his eye, Lin gasped.

"How is this possible?" Lin looked away from the glass. "There's a fox at the far end of the pasture...."

"It's a kind of magic," Ash said. "People will try to take these from you, so I recommend you don't show it to anyone unless you trust them."

Lin closed the scope and let it hang from the lanyard as he hugged Ash about the waist. "Do you have to go?"

"Yes, I must go. I've made promises. Duties to fulfill. I need to return some items to an old friend." He gently stroked Lin's hair. "Will you take good care of your mother until I visit again?" Lin's head snapped up at that. He didn't attempt to hide his tears or the smile on his face.

"You'll visit? Really?" Then he blurted, "I've got to check on the chickens...." He ran out the door wiping his eyes on his sleeves.

Holly was descending the stairs from the loft. Lin had seen her coming.

She didn't speak. She walked up to Ash, laid her cheek on his chest, and held him. After a few minutes, she looked up into his eyes.

"Did you mean it? What you said about coming back. Or were you just making Lin feel better?"

"I hear the Winter Solstice festival is nice." He softly kissed her. He breathed her in and the magic that steamed from her, like it was the only air in the world worth breathing.

Dunn's Arrow

"If you had been better managing your coins, we would not have had to sell the horses," Dunn said as he notched his favorite lucky arrow. "Besides, you've gotten too fat in the saddle, my friend."

Hollis adjusted his pack. "At least the summers are mild in the North Forest. I so love the shade. The trees are so tall and straight here. I don't know why that town has not harvested half of them for ship masts."

"Then, you place no stock in the haunted stories about this forest?" Dunn began scanning the woods to each side of the path for deer. "It's why they never come here. Except to travel straight through."

"Just stay on the path. Woods like this are the easiest to get lost in." Hollis looked into the gloom. There was no undergrowth. There was just a maze of tree trunks that would cause you to lose sight of the path in a few dozen paces. "Simple forest town folk like that would sooner believe in ghostly legends luring their sons to their doom, rather than consider that their sons were idiots and got lost."

"Well, parts of their story are genuine. With canopy so high and no lower limbs, the sky is hidden." Dunn said. "And no moss. Get lost in there, and you have no idea what way you're going. I bet it gets especially dark in there as well at night. But, at least it's full of game."

Dunn knelt to look at deer sign in the path. There was a fresh pile of dung pellets. Automatically he began to follow the trail into the woods straight where the road started to bend.

"Stay on the path, Dunn," Hollis whispered as he looked to make sure he was still on it. "The ghosts might lure you away with thoughts of venison."

Dunn was only ten paces into the trees when he held his hand up for silence. Dunn knew Hollis had seen this before. It was Dunn's own type of magic, so Hollis froze as he had been taught. Movement is what attracted the eye of the hunted. Their deep green cloaks and tunics would hide them.

Dunn heard the sound again. Footfalls. He didn't move anything but his eyes. Glimpses of massive antlers moved slowly through the gloom at a steady, predictable pace. He moved to profile his aim, his back directly to Hollis as he raised his bow in preparation to draw. The beautifully made arrow with its perfect barbed and bladed point would once again provide a feast or be lost or broken in these haunted trees. It was his favorite. It always found its mark.

The barb tracked the glimpses but revealed no clear shot. Slowly his whole body turned with the arrow as he drew it to his ear. His aim was drawn like gravity to its heart as he waited for the shot.

Then she was there.

Her eyes were wide with fear and pleading for help. Her hands extended toward him as if she were drowning. Then he suddenly realized his cruel arrowhead was aimed at her heart.

He blinked. As if to make sure she was real. The light in the forest changed. The sun above must have emerged from behind a cloud. The sun fell on her face as he lowered the bow, and she began it cry.

Her hands covered her face, and she dropped to her knees as her shoulders shook with the sobs. Dunn ran the thirty paces to her and could see her skirts were filthy and torn. Her hair was deep red. A color he had never seen before but reminded him of something he couldn't remember.

"Miss." Dunn tried to reassure her, "I won't hurt you. Are you alright?"

She looked up at him, towering over her. Her eyes were pleading. She choked out the words, "I've been lost in this forest for so long…."

"Dunn…" He heard Hollis call to him as she collapsed toward him. He dropped his bow and caught her. Kneeling, he gently turned her as she fainted in his arms. "Dunn…" the word was farther away.

When he turned back, he could not see Hollis or the path. But, through the trees to his right, he could see a portion of a chimney and the smoke from it.

Why could I not smell the smoke? The breeze in the forest hid as much as the trees. She must have come from there. He thought.

As he carried her there, he counted his paces. The cottage was only perhaps fifty paces total away from the path. He heard Hollis again, fainter still.

"Dunn!"

It can't be helped. He knew Hollis. He'd stay put and wait for him. He knew he could backtrack his footprints to the path.

The stone cabin was tiny. It had a steep thatch roof and a single leaded paned window. The door stood open like a gaping maw as he approached and entered. It contained only a single piece of furniture—a large ornately carved bed.

Dunn laid her on the bed, and she began to stir as he placed his hand on her forehead to check for fever. She was so beautiful, so perfect. It was like the light gathered around her.

Dunn looked to the door as he faintly heard Hollis in the distance.

"Dunn. No. What are you doing…."

When had night fallen?

The fireplace had a fire blazing with it. Candles in glass jars lined up on top of the low rafters, the mantle, and other shelves.

Did I make that fire? Did I set those candles? He thought.

When he reached up for one of the jars, he saw that his left arm was tense and shaking. He realized he was on the verge of a cramp in his right shoulder. He rose to go and speak to Hollis, to reassure him. But when he stood at the edge of the bed, she grasped his hand. Her eyes begged him to stay.

When had she undressed? How could all these quilts and sheets and pillows be so white and clean?

"Please. Don't leave me here." She begged him.

He sat again on the edge of the bed. "How long have you been here?"

"So very long…." She relaxed back. "I was so lost." She drew his shaking left hand to place on her sternum.

Her skin was so beautiful. Dunn felt so sleepy.

Dunn told her the story, "In the forest town of Greenwood, they have an Inn called the Loaf and Ladle. We heard a story there about a ghost of a red-haired witch in these haunted woods. Young men would bring her gifts, but she would always send them away. They would become lost and die in this forest."

"Please stay with me. Hold me." She was pleading.

"Dunn…" in the distance.

It was all a fog in his mind. Dunn wondered if he had a fever.

How had he gotten undressed? Their arms and legs tangled beneath the silken sheets and thick quilts. He felt heady, as if he had been drinking for hours. Then she was straddling him. Sitting up and on full display in all her perfection.

He wanted her.

She held his shaking left hand to her heart as she whispered. "Finally. The gift I have sought for an age…"

Then the mist of illusion ripped away like cobwebs.

Dunn stood in the forest. He was holding his bow with a shaking hand as his eyes focused on the singing string.

"NOO…" Hollis screamed as he tackled Dunn too late. "What have you done?"

The two men froze where they landed as they both turned to look at her.

She was staring down at the arrow in the center of her chest. Blood began to spread as she stumbled toward them. She fell to her knees, and Dunn caught her in his arms.

"Thank you," she whispered. "This was the gift I waited for…" But, unfortunately, she never finished the sentence as she turned to dust as the arrow fell to the ground.

Suddenly winds surrounded them. The sky grew brighter. It was the early evening. The forest seemed to change, and now they could see the ruins of a small cottage thirty paces away. The thatch was mostly gone. The exposed rafters mimicked the ribs of skeletons that littered the ground around the cottage's ruin. Bone fingers still held jewelry, a silver hairbrush, tattered silks, and gold coins in rotting velvet bags.

They collected what treasures they could easily carry. They left half behind. Dunn and Hollis never returned to the forest town of Greenwood. They never spoke of the origins of their new wealth. They never laughed again at stories told in Inns about cursed witches.

He left a gift to mark her grave—Dunn's favorite arrow.

Afterward

This collection is a warmup for a fantasy novel that I have planned for the future.

The characters in these stories will be featured in that novel if the outline remains intact: Cass, Thorn, and Peck from *The Once Damned*. Ash and Hale from *Justice in the Mist*. And Dunn and Hollis from *Dunn's Arrow*.

It will take place a few years later. The vacuum created by the death of the Queen and the positioning of the ruling houses creates a series of conflicts that eventually drag in these characters.

Alas, there are four or five books in line before this one.

As my friend Tony likes to say, "Shut up and type faster, Monkey."

About the Author

Martin Wilsey is a full-time author and creator of the highly acclaimed and best-selling, *Solstice 31 Saga*.

Mr. Wilsey's first novel, *Still Falling*, was published on March 31st of 2015. Less than three years and over a half a million published words later, he retired from his career as a research scientist for a government-funded think tank. As a full-time science fiction writer, Mr. Wilsey still uses his research and whiteboard skills to keep the books flowing. He likes to put the science back into science fiction.

As a prolific blogger, Martin shares what he has learned on his journey as an indie published author. On his blog, he writes a weekly webcomic and shares his inspir-ations and views on life. In addition to writing, he has begun to expand efforts into publishing through Tannhauser Press, audio narration, and podcasting.

Mr. Wilsey has more projects than he has time.

Please feel free to email him and distract him even more.

He and his wife Brenda live in Virginia with their cats, Brandy and Bailey.

Email him or follow him on Social Media!

He just might kill you in his next novel...

Sign up for email notifications to get free stories and stay up-to-date on future projects. I promise to never share your information. I hate it when that's done to me. I also promise to never SPAM you.

MartinWilsey.com

ACKNOWLEDGMENTS

I have several people to thank for their help with this book. I will begin with my wife Brenda. Thank you for your patience as it appears, I go deaf while I'm writing. Thank you for all your feedback and ideas. And thank you for caring for me all through that horrible year, encouraging me to write to forget my pain and my loss.

Thanks go to my son Gray and daughter Cady. Thank you for making me proud of you. Thanks for making it so easy to be your dad.

Thanks go to David Keener and Donna Royston for their help editing. I know it was a lot of heavy lifting.

Look for Tannhauser Press Anthologies

THE
WITNESS-
PARADOX
A TIME TRAVELER
ANTHOLOGY
EDITED BY MARTIN WILSEY

Discover the Best-Selling Solstice 31 Trilogy

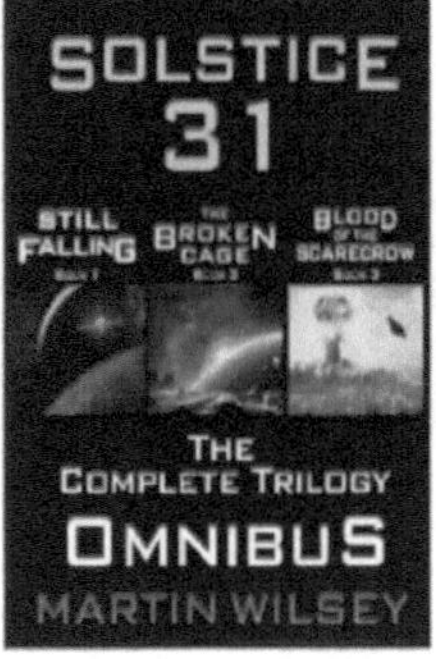

MARTIN WILSEY
BLOOD SKY
DREAMS
The Vampire Conspiracy
Book 2

CREDITS

Cover

"The Autumn Power," by Robin Fischer, licensed from BookCoverZone.

Stories

"Once Damned" © 2017 Martin Wilsey, originally published in *Fantastic Defenders*.

"Dunn's Arrow" © 2018 Martin Wilsey, originally published as "The Winter Archer" in *A Hanutingly Romantic Winter*.

"Justice in the Mist" © 2023 Martin Wilsey, originally published in *Fantastic Detectives*.

Images

Arrow Separator: Part of the "Hunting Arrows" image collection, by Tribaliumvanka, licensed from Deposit Photos.

Ax Separator: Part of the "Ancient Weapon" image collection, from losw, licensed from Deposit Photos.

Sword Separator: Part of the "Ancient Swords" image collection, licensed from Deposit Photos.

Title Page Dingbat: Part of "Set of Short Dividers," by Den Barbulat, licensed from Deposit Photos.

Chapter Dingbat: Part of "Set of Short Dividers," by Den Barbulat, licensed from Deposit Photos.